A LONG WAY TO PITT STREET

When conman Matthew Langley meets Matthew Lancing in a Hong Kong bar, he makes the most of this golden opportunity — at Lancing's expense. He murders Lancing, hides the body and assumes his identity, travelling back to England to claim Lancing's inheritance, which includes a substantial holding in a business. Two years later, Lancing's body is discovered, and Tom Leng comes from Hong Kong seeking Matthew Langley. When Leng's murdered body is discovered in Pitt Street, it is a case for Detective Inspector Sam Bawtry . . .

'Just a passing visit, purely social,' said Bawtry amiably.

Hodson grinned. 'Anybody who ever did a stint in the old 'B' Division always comes back. We had four in last week, all on pension these last ten years.'

'Well, I'm a fair way off that,' said Bawtry. 'How's everything?'

'On t'quiet side, the local Neds seem to be behaving themselves just at present. Mind you,' went on Hodson darkly, 'it'll not last. Lull before t'storm.'

'That's just your natural pessimism, Ben. You could be in for a long spell of nothing.'

'You're joking, you know that.'

'Happen I am. Any road, the lads wouldn't like it, sitting on their backsides in the pandas and never getting out.'

'Better than getting blisters on our feet like we used to. Not,' added Hodson, 'that these young chaps know much about *that.*'

One of the constables grinned, seemed about to make a crack but, remembering that Ben Hodson was a stickler for discipline, prudently decided not to.

Books by Douglas Enefer
in the Linford Mystery Library:

THE DEADLY STREAK
THE LAST LEAP
THE SIXTH RAID
LAKESIDE ZERO
ICE IN THE SUN
THE DEADLINE DOLLY

DOUGLAS ENEFER

A LONG WAY TO PITT STREET

Complete and Unabridged

LINFORD
Leicester

First published in Great Britain in 1972 by
Robert Hale Limited, London

First Linford Edition
published 2004
by arrangement with
Robert Hale Limited, London

The characters and events described in this
book are fictional and imaginary — but the
Liverpool background is, I hope,
uncompromisingly authentic.

British Library CIP Data

Enefer, Douglas, *1906* –
   A long way to Pitt Street.—Large print ed.—
Linford mystery library
   1. Detective and mystery stories
   2. Large type books
   I. Title
   823.9'14 [F]

   ISBN 1–84395–461–3

Published by
F. A. Thorpe (Publishing)
Anstey, Leicestershire

Set by Words & Graphics Ltd.
Anstey, Leicestershire
Printed and bound in Great Britain by
T. J. International Ltd., Padstow, Cornwall

This book is printed on acid-free paper

For
ALICE PRENDERGAST

1

It was exactly seven o'clock on the evening of 10 September when Bawtry parked his car and walked into the Marion Square and Oriel Road bridewell at one end of the vast new 'B' Division which scoops in all of Bootle and a massive slice of the north end of Liverpool.

Veteran cops like Joe Oldfield, now at Headquarters, who could remember pounding the old 'B' Division from the Everton Terrace and Prescot Street station were less than enthusiastic about the new territorial boundaries set up by the merging of the Liverpool and Bootle Forces and there was an 'in' joke which held that some of them couldn't find their way around without a beat book.

Sam Bawtry had worked in the old 'B' Division before he became a detective inspector attached to Headquarters C.I.D. and retained a nostalgic affection

1

for the area, privately regretting the widespread demolition and the soaring blocks of flats which had changed the top end of Great Homer Street almost out of recognition, banishing the street barrow women along with the characteristic bustling atmosphere he once knew. But, then, he regretted a lot of the things that just now were re-carving the face of the city he had come to love as if it were his own. He supposed it was inevitable in the context of the times, but he didn't have to like it, or not all of it.

These thoughts were stirring in his mind as he went through the doorway and stood blinking for a second while his eyes adjusted themselves to the sudden darkened transition from the blazing sunlight of the streets.

A voice said: 'Why, Sam — what brings you here?'

Bawtry walked up to the long counter. Ben Hodson, a uniformed sergeant, was behind it with a couple of constables who looked young enough to have just finished initial training out at Bruche.

Bawtry reflected that there were old-timers still in harness who viewed the increasing use of panda car patrols with mixed feelings, some even holding that young coppers simply liked riding around in cars and never saw half of what was going on. But the pandas gave rapid mobility, like the two-way pocket radios gave instant contact. Bawtry thought the pandas were fine but that there ought to be more men on the beat. There was no substitute for the uniformed man walking the streets, never had and never would be. The foot-slogging cop got to know people intimately, friends and foes alike, and no amount of mechanised mobility could do it. But there weren't enough men to go round. The police were below strength and up and down the country young chaps were leaving for better money than the service offered. There was something wrong with a country which couldn't or wouldn't pay for its own protection from the villains — and there were too many of *them* just now, for God's sake. Well, there were a lot of things wrong with the country, not least the mindless violence and the organised rise of anarchy, and one day the bill was going to come in.

In the last eleven months Bawtry himself had had three separate offers to join private security organisations at better money than he was likely to get even if he made superintendent's rank. He hadn't even considered them. Police work was his life, coming second to nothing except his love for the copper-headed girl who became Carol Bawtry after his lonely and sometimes embittered years of growing misogyny. Carol had wiped out all the bitterness, illuminating his life with the warmth of her personality and transforming it with her love, and he knew that he would quit the service if staying in it ever threatened the security of his marriage. He was thankful that the necessity for the choice had never arisen.

Ben Hodson, who was nearly a decade younger than Bawtry, lit a cigarette and said: 'Everything under control at Headquarters, then?'

'Pretty well. We're having a quiet time ourselves just now. It'll not last, as you say.'

'Never does,' said Hodson. 'One of the troubles is the new kind of villains who keep bobbing up. Not like the old days when you knew all the talent and where to find 'em. Makes the job harder.'

'Yes, it does. More interesting, though.'

Hodson fanned cigarette smoke with his right hand, looking at Bawtry's powerful physique; six feet of hard masculinity, no belly fat. He remembered when Bawtry was middleweight boxing champion of the Force and thought; this one's kept himself in trim, all right. But it was more than fitness. There were plenty of dedicated cops on the strength, but none had ever matched Sam Bawtry and he was lucky to have a wife who never moaned about it. What a woman Carol Bawtry was; a looker, too. Lucky Sam they called him, though he didn't know it. The best man at the old interrogation, nobody could chat up a suspect like Sam Bawtry; he had an almost uncanny feeling for the hidden truth, as though he could already see it, clear and certain, through the fog of lies and evasion. It was odd in a way, because he wasn't self-consciously tough, not like 'Tiger' Brooker. It was something else. Hodson, who had worked at various times with Bawtry, had sensed it — a driving compulsion not merely to put the villains down but to grasp what made them tick. Only the truly great detectives had this quality and Bawtry was high among their number, even if the top brass hadn't given him new promotion. Maybe they never would, not because he was unable to pass the examinations but because he played too many lone hands. Bawtry himself didn't mind. He liked what he was doing and was able to do it his own way, which might not be so easy if he went up another notch in the hierarchy. It was Brooker who had once said, without a trace of malice, 'If I die in the next five minutes they'll not put my shoes on your feet.' Well, it was likely true enough.

They fell into easy conversation about the divisional changes, hectic Saturday nights in the Prescot Street bridewell and the long-gone 'ghost' at the old Everton Terrace station. Bawtry thought: I'm getting sentimental in my old age.

Hodson started on another tack. 'Remember Bill . . . ' But he never finished the reminiscence.

A woman came through the doorway, an old woman with a wrinkled face ruddier than a cherry and a man's cap on her wispy grey hair.

Hodson said: 'What's to do, Biddy?'

'It's me bit o' brass, I had it in me shopping bag, I bin doing me week-end buying and called in at 'Grapes for me Guinness and now it's gone.'

'What, the Guinness?' asked Hodson facetiously.

Biddy McShann bridled. 'We don't pay slops to make jokes about a poor widow woman what's been robbed of her money!'

'Robbery is it, then?' Hodson pulled a sheet of foolscap paper towards him and picked up a pen. 'Just give us the details, Biddy.'

'I told you, dint I? Me money's gone. It was in me shopping bag while I waited for t'bus.'

'How much did you have in it — a pound or two, eh?'

'A hun'red it was . . . '

Hodson stared. 'A *hundred*!'

'Me savings, I allus carry them with me.'

'God Almighty,' roared Hodson. 'why didn't you put it in the bank?'

Biddy McShann plucked at the old-fashioned cameo brooch on her majestic bosom. 'Don't hold with banks, young man, I like to see the colour of me money.'

'Well, now you can't see it. Carrying all that brass about with you, it's asking for trouble.'

Bawtry interposed: 'D'you mind if I ask a question, Ben?'

'Not a bit.'

'Did anybody know you kept a lot of money on you, ma'am?'

The old woman eyed him dourly, up and down. 'Who're you, then?'

'Detective Inspector Bawtry, Headquarters Criminal Investigation Department,' intoned Hodson.

'I thought he were too well-dressed for a slop,' said Biddy.

'*Did* anybody know you kept a large

sum of money on you?' Bawtry persisted.

'D'yer think I'm daft, young man? I never told nobody, that is . . . '

'Yes?'

'I just remembered summat. I opened 'bag in the boozer, once it was. There were a young fella near me, but he went out first. He was at t'bus stop when I got there.'

'Describe him, ma'am.'

'Twenty-three or thereabouts. Wore them drainpipe pants, jeans they call 'em. Long hair, like they have these days — cissies.'

'What colour hair?' asked Hodson.

'Blond it was, nearly white and down to his shoulders . . . '

Hodson turned to one of the constables. 'Sounds like Whitey Malley — get after him, Fred, before he starts chucking that hundred quid about.'

'You know him?' demanded the old woman eagerly.

'We've had our beady eyes on him for a bit. He's a dipper, specialises in nicking handbags off ladies in shops and bus queues.' Hodson started writing, looked up and said: 'Mind you, we can't be sure, but if he's got your brass rest assured we'll get it back for you. Well, most of it, any road.'

'I should hope so,' snorted Biddy McShann.

'We do our best to justify the fat salaries the ratepayers give us,' said Hodson, poker-faced.

'What do I do, wait here?'

Hodson pointed to a door. 'Take a seat in there and we'll send you in a nice hot cuppa. Happen we'll send you on your way rejoicing before long.'

The old woman pulled the cap down further on her head and said: 'You're not so bad — for slops, that is.'

She went into the small room as Constable Raynes came in from the street.

Hodson said sharply: 'You're late on duty, P.C. 31.'

'Sorry, sarge. I had . . . ' The uniformed man, who was in his late thirties, looked uncomfortably at Bawtry.

'I'm just paying a social call, constable,' said Bawtry mildly.

11

Hodson eyed the officer bleakly: 'And don't lean on the bloody counter, 31. You've got a backbone, haven't you?'

Raynes stood up stiffly. 'I was a bit put about, I didn't think, some private bother . . . ' He looked worried and embarrassed in about equal proportions.

'Something wrong at home?' Hodson's hard tone had changed.

'It's that kid of mine, Alison. I'm bothered about her. We had a flaming row as I was about to come on duty.' Raynes hesitated. 'I don't like t'company she's getting into. She's only eighteen.'

'Well, keep her in order, then. You're head of the house, aren't you?'

'You haven't got any kids, sarge, have you?'

'What's that got to do with it?'

'They don't go for the big stick any more, not these days.' Raynes drew a hand down the side of his face. 'She's out all hours, comes in when she thinks fit — one bloody row after another and it makes no difference. I'm worried.'

Bawtry said: 'This company you say your daughter's keeping — what sort of company exactly?'

'Long-haired layabouts, in and out of coffee bars and even boozers.'

'Not every young fella with long hair is a layabout, constable.'

'I dare say, but she's young to be out the way she is and . . . '

'You had some words and it finished with her flouncing out of the house, is that it?'

'More or less, sir. She went out made up and dressed to the nines, if you can call what they wear these days being dressed.'

Bawtry felt for cigarettes, then decided not to. He had come down from forty a day to fifteen and had smoked ten of them so far. 'Try having a friendly chat, no shouting,' he said. 'If you think she may be knocking around with undesirables she ought to listen, particularly as you're in the Force.'

Raynes shrugged. 'That makes it worse, she seems to hate the fact that I'm a copper.'

There was truth in that, Bawtry reflected. The neighbours threw sidelong looks at you if you were in the police; it was as if there was a silent barrier between you and the people you were there to protect. Another reason for having more fellas on the beat; people got to know you, became friends. If there was trouble, real trouble, it was you they turned to; where else could ordinary people go?

'Well, have a try, Raynes,' he said.

'I will, sir.' Raynes went on quickly: 'Alison's a good kid, really, but she's headstrong and obstinate and it could land her in trouble. It's sort of got worse between us since my wife was killed in that accident three years ago. A girl needs her mother, especially at fifteen.'

'A father, too. You might've been a bit too much of the disciplinarian. Anyway, don't lose your temper with her next time, it never gets you anywhere.' Bawtry tipped his curly-brimmed hat slightly on his forehead. 'Well, I'll be off. Nice to have seen you, Ben.'

He went out to his car and started driving, slowly, though the early evening traffic was temporarily light, turning over what Raynes had told them. He was at the bottom of Byrom Street close to the Technical College when he saw the two-seater car parked outside a tobacconist's. A girl was in the passenger seat, a girl with medium-length dark hair and a slightly pointed face. She was Alison Raynes.

A youngish fellow with fanned-out sideboards and a light-weight grey suit with the wider lapels now back in style came out of the shop and slid down behind the wheel, tearing the transparent wrapper off a packet of twenty cigarettes.

Bawtry turned his own car in front and got out.

2

'Hello, Terry,' he said.

The pale face looked up at him, a face schooled to show as little as possible of its owner's thoughts; but the narrowed eyes were giving enough away.

'Yeh?'

'So you've got yourself a car since we last met.' Bawtry glanced at it, a four-year-old Triumph Spitfire. 'Bit of rust starting to show on the wings. Nice little job, though.'

Terry Byass put a cigarette in his mouth, lit it with exaggerated deliberation and let out a long stream of smoke. 'We're on our way — *do* you mind?'

'I might.' Bawtry splayed both hands on the side of the car, looking down at the girl, who was fiddling uncomfortably with her handbag. 'I believe you know me slightly, Miss Raynes.'

Her pointed chin tilted up. 'You're a cop, like my Dad, aren't you?'

'That's right, I've just been chatting with him.'

'Oh?'

'He's a bit worried about you.'

'Moaning, you mean? He's always on to me about one thing or another.'

'Happen he's fond of you, Miss Raynes. You're eighteen, aren't you?'

'Yes — what's that got to do with it?'

Bawtry said: 'This fella you're with is twenty-nine.'

'What of it?'

'Just that there's a discrepancy, and not only in age.'

'Drop dead!' said Terry Byass.

'Bit embarrassing for you if I did, right here,' answered Bawtry equably. 'On the other hand, not so embarrassing as some things.'

Alison Raynes said: 'What are you getting at, making remarks like that?'

'This fella's been inside,' said Bawtry. 'In prison. He's only been out of Walton three weeks.'

The girl started, then turned in her seat. 'Tell him he's a liar, Terry, you tell him that.'

Terry Byass blew smoke at his hands. Bawtry went on: 'Breaking and entering. Not the first time. Two years in Borstal when he was little more than your age. Three convictions since then.'

Terry Byass said: 'I done my time. You're not supposed to hound me, especially as I'm going straight.'

'That's fine, Terry — you keep it like that and I don't have to feel your collar again.'

Alison Raynes said, without looking up: 'You never said you'd been in . . . in prison.'

'I'm trying to go straight, I didn't want you to know, love.'

The girl's head jerked up, her eyes on Bawtry. 'You're like Dad — give a dog a bad name, never let up, that's how you all are.'

'I'm not hounding your boy friend because of his record, though I think a proper fella would've told you, Miss Raynes. There's something else.'

'What?'

Bawtry didn't answer directly. Instead,

he said: 'Have you been out with him before?'

'No, we only met today . . . '

'I'm glad,' said Bawtry. 'I mean I'm glad you haven't been out with him before.'

'Why, what're you getting at?'

'Tell her, Terry,' said Bawtry.

Terry Byass turned the key in the ignition and reached for the gear lever. Bawtry thrust a hand down and switched the engine off. 'I said tell her.'

'Don't know what you're on about . . . '

'I'll refresh your memory, then. It was while you were in Walton. You had to have treatment, hospital treatment.'

'Shut up, you stinking copper!'

Alison Raynes stared uncomprehendingly. 'What're you on about?'

'Terry knows.'

'Knows what?'

Bawtry looked down at them. 'All right, if he won't tell you, I will. He had to go to the VD clinic.'

Her face flooded with colour, then went white. 'You're lying, you're just saying it.'

'No, that's why I'm glad you haven't been with him, really been with him, Miss Raynes. I'll be brutal about it — Terry's had gonorrhoea.'

'Oh, dear God,' said Alison Raynes. 'It's not true, is it, Terry, it's not true?'

He didn't speak and she moved sideways, as if terrified of contact.

'Happen he's been cured, but he's had it, Alison,' said Bawtry. 'I had to tell you.'

Suddenly, she began trembling. Then, without a word, she swung the car door open and got out and went along the pavement, almost running.

Terry Byass sat without movement, as if frozen in the seat. His face twisted, like a silent snarl.

'One of these days I'll do you, copper,' he whispered.

★   ★   ★

Bawtry got back in his car and drove to Headquarters. He went up the three steps past *Inquiries*, down more steps into the courtyard and on into the C.I.D. section. An advance whiff of mild cigar smoke told him that Brooker was in residence with about forty minutes left before going off duty, which meant going to the pub and later, if he was running true to form, to the Press Club. There had been a time when the Chief Detective Inspector hadn't been a big drinking man, any more than Bawtry was, but that was before Marion Brooker walked out on him on a bitter night, never to return. If colleagues often wondered what had become of her they kept the thought to themselves; not even Brooker's superiors cared to raise the subject in his hearing. Only to Bawtry, in a moment of unexpected self-revelation, had Brooker confided the background of his wrecked emotional life and Sam had told no one apart from Carol. Meanwhile, Brooker still had the house out at Knotty Ash which he had shared with Marion Brooker for a dozen years, though it would be less than accurate to say he lived in it. Home was where he slept, bathed and breakfasted; though he had kept everything neat, even the gardens, doing it on off-duty days. The rest of the time he spent working and drinking, but nobody had seen him even half-cut or denied his professional efficiency.

But at this time of the evening he was still without a whisky breath because he never started drinking until he was free of duty. His face, which looked as if it had been carved out of sandstone, creased in a grin of welcome.

'Hello, Sam. Are you buying me one shortly or going straight home?'

'The latter, I think. Sorry.'

'I'd be going straight home myself if I had someone like Carol waiting.'

'I've just been chatting-up Terry Byass,' said Bawtry.

Brooker's eyes flickered. 'That young bastard — what's he been up to?'

'Nothing criminal, at least nothing that I know of.' Bawtry explained briefly.

Brooker took the cheroot from his hard mouth. 'Well, you saved Raynes's girl from getting the clap — unless, of course, they cured him in hospital. I hope she's grateful.'

'Scared would be more like it.'

'Aye. Well, a good scare does no harm.

Better than all her old fella's ranting at her. But what the bloody hell is a cop's daughter doing with a villain like Terry Byass?'

'She didn't know he was a villain until I told her. Raynes says she's difficult. Among other things, she doesn't like her father being a policeman.'

'That's been known before, more's the pity. We tend to live in a sort of private world, isolated from the civvies. It wasn't always like that and it's not because we want it, either. Damn it all, Sam, we're here to help the civvies, that's what police work is about.'

'Yes,' said Bawtry.

'Terry Byass,' mused Brooker. 'Smash and grab, breaking and entering, being found on enclosed premises — you name it, he's done it, more than twice, and we haven't caught him every time. He's only been out weeks. Where'd he get the money to buy a car?'

'Proceeds of previous crimes, perhaps.'

'H'm. How about his old fella?'

'Nothing we know about.'

Toby Byass was in his middle fifties, a

cracksman with a record going back all of three decades. Nothing on the crime sheet for half that time, result of a mixture of cunning and luck. Now working regularly at his original trade of rigger, and if he spent more money than most riggers that was because he had plenty salted away, happen enough not to have to blow safes again. Not yet, anyway.

'Toby's knocking the hard stuff,' said Brooker. He made a fleeting grin. 'I knock it myself, but not the way he does. I ran across him in a pub off Lime Street, two or three times as a matter of fact. The last time he was having the hair of the dog and he needed it. He'd got the shakes, couldn't keep his hands still.'

'Well, that ought to keep him out of trouble, if nothing else does,' remarked Bawtry.

The wall clock showed eight p.m. and they strolled together through the main office, free for what was left of the evening.

Oldfield was on desk duty, not due off until the witching hour; the time of the big rota change-over, one mob going off as another came on, the traditional best of all times for the villains. He nodded amiably, a large man with wiry grey hair and a heavy lined face. He had been on the strength more years than anybody could count; in fact, there were young constables who privately said that Joe Oldfield must be at least a hundred.

Two of them came in through the big doorway, Collins and Armiston from one of the cars. They looked troubled and Bawtry, who noticed this, said sharply: 'What's up?'

'Car crash out at Deysbrook Lane near the new multi-storey flats. Tom Raynes's girl, run over.'

'Christ,' said Bawtry. 'She's not . . . '

'No, just injured.' Bert Collins fingered the peak of his cap. 'Don't know details yet. We got a message through to the Oriel Road bridewell for Tom Raynes. He's at the casualty station.'

'Who was driving the car?'

'A woman, a Mrs. Lancing, Della Lancing. Doesn't seem to have been her fault. The girl stepped off t'pavement right in front of her, according to eye-witnesses.'

'Where is she? The lady driver, I mean.'

'WPC 30 is with her, in the interview room, taking a statement.'

'I'd like a word with her,' Bawtry said.

Bert Collins looked curious and Bawtry added: 'I was talking to Alison Raynes earlier tonight. There's something I'd like to ask Mrs. Lancing.'

He went through to the interview room. Della Lancing was sitting at the plain table facing Joyce Gregson, the WPC. Bawtry took in the stylish clothes, the excellent figure, the subtly-applied make-up on the kind of face that could turn heads without the need to be conventionally pretty. Age anywhere between thirty and forty, probably closer to the former.

Without preamble Bawtry said who he was and asked: 'Was this young lady running, Mrs. Lancing?'

'No, she was standing on the edge of the pavement and just stepped straight off it, suddenly. I trod on everything, but I couldn't stop in time to avoid her, not at that distance.'

'Did she seem preoccupied?'

'I really couldn't say, inspector.'

Bawtry thought: God Almighty, if I hadn't chatted her up it wouldn't have happened, she'd still be all right. She would also have been with Terry Byass. Just the same, Bawtry felt self-reproach. He had acted as he thought right; well, it *was* right, but that didn't stop him feeling badly about it, almost as if he had sent her straight into the car.

He heard himself saying, mechanically: 'About what speed were you driving at, ma'am?'

'I wasn't looking at the clock, but not more than twenty, I should think, when I saw her step off. I braked and didn't really hit her hard. I suppose it was the way she fell.'

The door opened and Collins said: 'Fractured forearm, according to the house surgeon at t'hospital.'

Della Lancing made a small shiver. 'I've never had an accident before, it was . . . well, unnerving.'

'I take it you were on your way home,

Mrs. Lancing?' Bawtry asked the question without really caring; it didn't matter where she was going.

There was a small pause. 'Yes,' she said.

Bawtry nodded. He was driving home before it struck him that there was something about the way she had spoken the single word. But he had no notion what it was.

3

Della Lancing had turned the bronze Cortina 1300 into the gravelled drive of their house off Walton Hall Avenue when she saw Matt's car, a year-old Humber Sceptre, in the double garage with the sliding door up. The sight of it was almost like a physical impact. For a long moment she was almost too petrified to get out. She had been certain he was over in Manchester; business conference at the Queen's, not coming back till late. 'Don't expect me much before midnight, darling,' he had said over breakfast.

That was why she had gone out about tea-time. Previously it had always been in the afternoon — a matinée performance, Charles called it in his deep, smooth voice. Not that Charles Bamer had been the only one, not by half a dozen in the last eighteen months. She had never been in love with any of them, consciously sidestepping any real emotional involvement. Just nice boy friends, all but one of them married; looking for extra-marital adventures. For them, too, it had to be a matinée, in a hotel with a room booked for the night, but not used at night. Charles, who was the bachelor exception, would take her to his flat, a luxury flat in a smart block, not one of the multi-storey things, though it wasn't far from them.

'If your old man's away why not drop in rather later?' he had said. 'You could be on your way before eight, if you're worrying in case he gets back a bit early.'

So she had driven there just before five, letting herself in with a key he had given her. A nice place it was, all very mod with a radio gramophone and a stack of classic pop albums — Frank Sinatra, Bobby Darin, Billy Eckstein, Peggy Lee. 'Our kind of music, sweetheart,' said Charles gaily. 'Sort of grown-up, eh?'

He was grown-up in other ways: forty years old and handsome with it, suits from Savile Row, charm by the ton, ran his own shipping agency, clearing four thousand a year after tax plus expenses.

Della supposed he had had more women than the sober and righteous had had Sunday dinners and that she was no more than the latest in the line. She didn't mind, she had the same idea about men. Besides, she wasn't looking for the righteous, though she preferred men to stay sober; it was so maddening if they took a few drinks too many and couldn't rise to the occasion.

Two hours she had been there. Music in plenty, champagne in moderation. A little romantic play-acting before they abandoned themselves to each other. Charles was the best of the lot. Not that she wanted their liaison to last; a few weeks, perhaps a couple of months, no more. Her responses to him were wholly physical, nothing of her true self was even remotely committed. He probably hadn't so much as glimpsed what she was really like, the real woman behind the façade. Well, that was all right, she didn't want either of them to probe below the surface of easy promiscuity.

'See you on Tuesday, then — afternoon next time,' she had said as she lightly touched her boldly attractive face with make-up at his dressing-table.

'I'll count the moments, sweetheart.' He wouldn't, but neither would she. Still, it *was* something to look forward to, a naughty little break in the monotony of dutiful domesticity.

Then she was driving home, not fast, lots of time — time to look at the television when she got there and be able to tell Matt which programme she enjoyed most. Even the chance of being spotted in this part of the city was slight enough to discount; her friends were unlikely to be there any more than they'd suppose she was. Just the same, she kept an alert eye open: then that slip of a girl stepped right off the pavement in front of her. God Almighty, I could have killed her; but she had crash-braked, enough to avoid a really bad impact. Suppose the crash *had* been fatal? Della shivered, though the night was warm. There'd have been an inquest, evidence to the coroner about what part of town she was driving in — she'd have had a hell of a job explaining that away to Matt.

Well, the girl had only collected a fractured shoulder and as she had stepped in front of the car there wouldn't be a court case. Della breathed relief as she turned her car into the drive of the £14,000 house with the fine mansard roof and the five bedrooms and two bathrooms and separate lavatories coyly inscribed *His* and *Hers*. Everything was going to be all right.

Then she saw Matt's car . . .

For what seemed like a minor age she sat there, literally unable to move, her mouth suddenly dry, her mind a whirl of near-frantic thought. She had told Matt she was going to have a quiet day at home, nursing an incipient cold. Only she hadn't got any kind of cold, except the chill of fear.

She pulled herself together. Good God, I'm being a fool. All I have to do is say I felt better and fancied a run in the car. Yes, but where? Just a quiet run because it was a nice evening; I don't even have to tell him where I'm supposed to have driven, do I? Besides, he wouldn't ask. He'd never so much as suspected what she had been getting up to these last eighteen months, had he?

In fact, she had started playing around within six months of their marriage. That was all it had taken to reach the frontiers of boredom; she ought never to have married, she wasn't the type to make a go of it. That was what she told herself. In fact, she had never really tried. She supposed she had expected too much; a sort of perpetual honeymoon, lots of love and gay parties and seats in the orchestra stalls and long holidays in the Mediterranean sun. She was realistic enough to understand that no marriage could be exactly like that. It wasn't lack of money. They had a beautiful home, two cars, smart clothes, domestic help, everything she wanted except excitement. Just the same, she hadn't set out to cheat on Matt. It had simply happened, one of those things. She had driven into town and was having coffee in a restaurant when a good-looking fellow came in.

He hesitated at her table and said: 'Is this chair occupied, by any chance?'

She smiled, shaking her head. He sat

down, facing her. That was how it began. A casual exchange of looks, then not quite so casual. She knew intuitively what he was doing: undressing her with his eyes and wondering what the chances were. But all that actually happened, after some of the most crushingly dull small-talk she could ever remember, was that he said: 'I drop in here most mornings about this time. We might meet again. Tomorrow perhaps?'

'Perhaps,' she said.

What a bloody bore he was! Good looking and knew it, but a right bloody bore. She hadn't really meant to be there the next day, but when the time came she was there and so was he, waiting. Phil Edgeley he said he was. Married man, he made no bones about it. He seemed different this time, talked better and more easily. Why was that? Quite suddenly, she understood: he was more sure of himself — or, rather, more sure of her. Perhaps he hadn't really expected her to show up, but she had and the fact of it had made him more articulate.

They went to a bar near Ranelagh

Street, had three drinks and a pub lunch and at ten minutes past two in the afternoon he unlocked the door of a double bedroom in a quiet hotel. He closed it behind them and said, smiling: 'You've not played an away date before, have you?'

She shook her head wordlessly.

'I can tell. Don't worry, nobody'll know, darling.'

She laughed shakily. 'You booked this room in anticipation, didn't you?'

'In hope.'

'What if I hadn't turned up?'

He made a careless shrug. 'I'd have parted with eighty-two and six for nothing, that's all.'

'Were you glad when you saw me again?'

'Not just glad, half mad with desire.' He pulled her towards him, unresisting, stripping the clothes from her as they kissed. His voice was a parched rustle, 'I'll cover you with kisses and gobble you up, like a delicious treat.' Minutes later they were locked together on the bed, no more words. Matt had never made it last that long.

After Phil there were others. And now she was coming home to find Matt there when he should have been over in Manchester, not coming back until midnight. But the moment of freezing panic had gone and there was a reason. She was in command of herself now, strolling up to the front door with her lips pursed on a snatch of song, putting the key in the lock and calling out: 'Matt, you're home early — what a lovely surprise!'

He came down the wide hall, a fine figure of a man with a smooth, slightly sallow face and blue eyes under bushy brows.

'Hello, Della,' he said.

'Why didn't you ring . . . ' She checked herself in midsentence.

He snapped lights on. There was something in his face, something especially in his eyes. A small alarm gonged in her mind.

'I did,' he said.

'Oh?'

'Before I left, it would be an hour and a

37

half ago, I thought you weren't going out.'

She dropped her beige car coat on the ottoman. 'The cold didn't develop and I got a bit restless and went out for a drive.'

'Did you enjoy it?'

'Well, it was just a run in the car.'

'I didn't mean that,' he said.

'I . . . I don't . . . ' She fumbled the words out.

He came close up, looking down at her. 'I meant did you enjoy having it off with whoever the latest boy friend is.'

She could feel her heart thudding like a swinging brick. She went cold, icy cold, stretching her hands to stop them shaking.

He went back along the hall and said quietly: 'Come into the lounge, Della.'

She followed him, trying to still the panic in her mind. He knew . . . for God's sake, he *knew* . . . how, how? What did it matter how he knew?

Matt Lancing poured two whiskies. 'You look as if you could use a drink, darling.' What was he going to do? She didn't know, couldn't even begin to guess.

Then he was speaking again; calmly, as

if they were talking about the weather. 'I thought you were up to something, darling. I thought it first some months ago when I rang up several times and you weren't in and when I got home you didn't crack-on you'd been out. If you'd had the nous to pitch me a tale about going out shopping — anything — I'd probably never have known.'

She drank half the whisky and almost at once stopped feeling petrified. Who said having a drink didn't help to straighten you up? Not too many, though. But she still wasn't equal to speech. What can I say, anyway?

Matt lit a cigarette and went on: 'That was the first mistake you made. There were others — little things you never considered like having gin on your breath when the bottle we keep hadn't gone down. One or two other things, small things taken singly, only they weren't isolated.' He expelled a stream of smoke and fanned it with a hand. 'After a bit I decided to do something.'

'You had me *watched*?' Her voice was incredulous.

'Nothing so crude, darling. I suspected something, but I don't set private detectives on my own wife. No, I did the watching myself. Only once. Today, if you must know. And that was just by chance.'

'So you lied about going over to Manchester.'

'No, the meeting was put off at the last minute, that's what I meant about seeing you by chance. I had some business in town and I caught sight of you going into that block of flats, the one your boy friend has.' Matt Lancing laughed, not pleasantly. 'I even know him — Charles Bamer, a well-known chaser, specialises in married women. Or did you imagine you were the first?'

'No.' The word came out almost savagely. How dared he make fun of her!

'I don't know how long you've been having me on, darling . . .'

'You can stop calling me darling,' she said.

For a moment he stood still, looking directly at her. Then: 'Yes, it's not the right word, is it? Not any more. You bloody bitch, you!' His hand moved as he spoke, the flat of it hitting her across the side of the face.

Della Lancing staggered back. A reddening patch showed against the drained whiteness of her skin. She stopped with the small of her back against the big upholstered settee.

'If you ever touch me again I'll make you sorry for it,' she whispered.

He was staring at his hand, almost as if unwilling to believe what he had done. Then he said unsteadily: 'I didn't intend that, but you asked for it, didn't you? How many others have you been to bed with?'

She laughed, a short mirthless sound. 'Six, if you must know.'

'In God's name, why?'

'Don't bring God into it. Calling on your Maker doesn't exactly become you.'

'I've given you no cause. I've been a good husband to you, haven't I?'

'Now you're talking like the injured party in a glossy magazine serial, and *that* doesn't suit you, either. You'll be asking next what have you done to deserve this.'

'Well, what *have* I done?'

'There doesn't have to be anything,' she said coolly.

His long mouth tightened, making a downward curve. 'You mean you just like being had?'

'You can think what you like.'

'You don't leave me any alternative. Indiscrimiate shagging . . . '

'Don't use words like that to me, Matt. Besides, I'm not indiscriminate. I do the choosing.'

A bitter sound came from him. 'You cheap bitch — fellows like Charles Bamer, they spend half their time looking for easy pushovers.'

She put a cigarette in her mouth and lit it with hands no longer shaking. 'I like men, will that do then?'

Slowly, he said: 'I'm seeing you for the first time, or a part of you I never knew existed until now.'

'Well?'

'I thought you loved me.'

'I liked you enough to marry you, I paid you that compliment. I'm sorry it didn't last, but don't ask me to be sorry for what I've done because I'm not.'

He stared, as if unwilling to accept the implication of her words. 'You mean you're going *on* with it?'

'I'm going to live my own life exactly as I choose, Matt.'

His hand balled itself into a fist.

'Hit me just once more and I'll make you more sorry than you can imagine,' she said.

The fist unwound, hanging limply at his side. 'I could divorce you,' he said tightly.

'You haven't got enough evidence.'

'You're forgetting I followed you to Bamer's flat — his private entrance, in fact.'

'I'm surprised you didn't burst in doing the outraged husband act, then.'

'I almost did, but getting into a fist fight with your boy friend wasn't going to help.'

'No, and you wouldn't have liked the publicity, would you? Come to think of it, you wouldn't like the publicity of the divorce court, either.'

'No, I wouldn't!' His voice rose. 'So from now on you're going to behave yourself, do you hear?'

'Don't yell at me, Matt. Now I'll tell *you* something. From now on we're going to live separate lives with no recriminations, no questions asked and no answers given.'

'If you think I'll agree to that you've picked the wrong man, Della.'

'You've no choice,' she said calmly. 'I know too much about you.'

He had been about to move, but now he stood without movement, without words.

'I found it out a little while ago. I've kept it to myself, all this time I've said nothing. But I *know*.'

'What?' He tried to make the question a sneer.

'The one thing you can't afford to have bandied about, the one thing that would ruin you.'

'You — .' He used a word she had never heard from him.

Her face coloured. 'That's the real you coming out, isn't it?'

He made a travestied smile. 'As a matter of fact, it isn't. Perhaps you still don't know me.'

'Perhaps neither of us really knows the other.'

'I think I do — now.' He poured himself a fresh drink. 'You don't seriously expect to go on living in this house, putting on a nicely-nicely marital front to our friends — not after *this*, do you?'

'Why not? It's been done before.'

'It's not going to be done by me,' he said savagely.

'You don't have any choice.'

'I ought to kill you,' he said.

'Yes, and not simply because I've had some nice boy friends. But you won't.'

'Don't try me.'

She mashed her unfinished cigarette in a glass tray. 'You won't because I've made damned sure you daren't, Matt.'

His head jerked round at her.

'I've put everything I know in writing. The Lancing file. You'd better keep your fingers crossed that I never have a fatal accident in the car, because then it'd be found.'

He almost jumped across the room. Her voice stopped him in his tracks. 'It's not in the house, darling. Do you think I'm a complete idiot?'

Matt Lancing came back, slowly. He looked at his untasted drink, picked it up and drained the glass. He put it down on the table with a small rattle, breathing out through his mouth.

'I don't claim to know everything,' Della said, 'but I think I know enough, including the numbers I copied from a list I found in your desk. I had to guess what they mean, but I think I've come close to the truth.'

He stood there looking at her, his face ravaged.

'It's all in a place you can't get at,' she said. 'All locked up in safety deposit D.L. 5 at the International Commercial Bank.'

'I ought to kill you now,' Matt Lancing whispered.

'Not now, not ever, darling,' she said.

4

Bawtry drove to the hospital next day, immediately after the morning conference. If Alison Raynes was pleased to see him she was hiding the fact with an actress's skill.

He stood by the side of the bed with his hat in one hand. 'How are you, Miss Raynes?'

'I'm all right.'

'You could've been killed, you know.'

'Why, do you care?'

'Yes. Also your Dad.'

'All he cares about is trying to run my life for me,' she said bitterly.

Bawtry looked at her, propped up against the pillows, her left arm in a cage. 'Have you spoken to him?'

'He's spoken to me.'

'I didn't ask you that.'

'So you didn't. All right, then, I haven't — or only a few words.'

Bawtry said deliberately: 'You're a

bloody little fool.'

Colour flooded her pale face. Her mouth opened, but before she could get words out he went on: 'Hasn't it got into your thick head that your Dad might've thought you were getting involved with dubious characters?'

'I don't want to talk about it.'

'Meaning you don't like the truth. Well, few of us do, but we have to face up to it if we're going to live with ourselves. Tell me one thing — have you ever been with a fella, really been with one?'

'You've no right to come here asking things like that,' she flared.

'*Have* you?'

'No — not proper, anyway. What if I had?'

'You'd have to live with the knowledge of it.'

'It's not a crime to go with a boy.'

'I didn't say that. But would you have told your father?'

'I'd tell him nothing, he wouldn't understand.'

'For God's sake, do you think your old fella doesn't know anything about life?'

'All he knows is the crummy side of it.'

'He knows you, Miss Raynes.'

'He's a copper.'

'So am I.'

'Yes, you are.'

'As to knowing the crummy side of life — what damned side of it do you think Terry Byass knows?'

She winced, not with the pain in her arm. 'I didn't know he . . . '

'Your old fella was trying to steer you away from undesirables like Terry Byass. You might at least give him credit for that, don't you think?'

'You don't understand, do you?' Her mouth went into a long, tight line. 'Well, you wouldn't, you're too old — you don't understand us.'

'The young, you mean?'

She shrugged.

'I've been young, you know,' said Bawtry mildly.

'Things were different then, weren't they?'

'Not some of the basic things. That's a mistake all you kids make, thinking nobody before your time ever wanted to make love or start a revolt or had rows with their parents.'

For the first time something that was almost a smile moved on her face, transforming it. 'I just can't imagine you having a dust-up with your old fella,' she said.

'We had several.'

'What did he do, then?'

'Took his belt off and gave me a bit of a leathering.'

'Why, what had you been up to?'

'You've no right to ask questions like that,' Bawtry mimicked.

She laughed outright. 'I bought that all right, didn't I? Go on, though — what did you do?'

'Stayed out late with some other lads after he told me I had to be in by nine-thirty.'

'That's what my Dad told *me*.'

'If you'd been a boy perhaps he'd have given you a bit of a leathering.'

'Happen he should have, anyway. It'd have been better than him keeping on at me, everlasting nattering away. That's what made me do it, if you want to know.'

'You must've been up to something in the first place for him to start on you.'

'Only dolling myself up and going out, but the way he kept on moaning made me do it all the more. Then it . . . well, it sort of grew.'

'I can understand that.'

'I thought you were on Dad's side.'

'I'm on his side in the sense that he wanted to protect you. I don't necessarily agree with his way of going about it.'

'If you were my Dad what would you have done?' she asked mischievously.

Bawtry smiled. 'Chatted you up.'

'Only not in the same way?'

'Probably not.'

'Try to get on my right side, wouldn't you?'

'Happen I would, Alison.'

'So it's Alison now, is it?'

'I think so, don't you?'

She looked at him for a moment without speaking. Then she said: 'Yes. I like you, I didn't think I would, but now I do.'

'That's fine, then.'

'You know, if my Dad hadn't got all

51

het-up with me I wouldn't have done what I did.'

'Parents often have trouble getting through to their children. Sometimes it's easier for an outsider.'

'I don't see why.'

'You will.'

'What's that mean?'

'When you're married and have children of your own.'

'I don't know that I want to be wed. Running a house and washing shirts and changing nappies. Dead boring.'

'You'll change your mind, Alison.'

'When I meet Mister Right?' she mocked.

'Some day he'll come along, like the song says. A nice hard-working young fella who loves you.'

'Not one like Terry Byass?'

'No, not like him or any of his kind.'

She moved slightly against the high pillows. 'I'll tell you something. I didn't like him much even before you told me . . . what you told me. I was just doing it to spite me Dad.'

'Not a good reason for agreeing to go

out with a boy, is it?'

'No, it isn't, but I was mad at the way things were going at home.'

'So you let him pick you up?'

'Well, it wasn't quite like that. I'd seen him around in places I go to. You know, coffee bars and pop music sessions and all that. I could tell he was interested.'

'You wouldn't be the only one he was interested in.'

'Now you're being old-fashioned. Didn't you ever go with girls? I mean before you were old . . . oh, I didn't mean it like that.'

'That's all right. I'm forty-seven, which is practically doddering from where you're sitting.'

'Did you, though?'

'What, go with girls?'

She nodded.

'I had my moments,' said Bawtry. There had been several girls he had gone out with in his teens. Years later there was Laura. By that time he was forty and happen it wasn't a good age at which to fall in love for the first time. Then, on a bitter night in midwinter, she had left him

53

a farewell note — and only hours later she was dead, killed outright when the Jag driven by Rod Carnaby wrapped itself round some traffic bollards on the East Lancashire dual carriageway. Bawtry thought: it's like history repeating itself almost. Carnaby was a hook, the same as Terry Byass. When he crashed the car the impact flung him out through the burst-open driving door and he landed unhurt. In the next six years Bawtry lived in lonely and increasingly embittered isolation, occupied only by work — until Carol walked into his life and changed everything, for ever.

Suddenly, he was aware that Alison Raynes was looking directly at him. 'You were a long way off just then,' she said.

'Just remembering something.'

'You looked proper grim and then you looked . . . sort of happy.'

'You're very observant, Alison.'

'I'm a cop's daughter,' she said, without resentment now.

Without having thought about it, he said: 'Happen you'd make a good WPC.'

'That's right, I might.' She eyed him

again. 'I owe you something, don't I?'

Bawtry grinned. 'You don't have to put a uniform on to square it.'

'I've been lying here thinking about things,' she said. 'About everything, I mean. Dad and me and what I've been doing. I was heading for trouble, wasn't I? I knew I was getting in with the wrong crowd. I didn't even like what I was up to. It was just that I was mad at the way things were going at home.'

Bawtry thought of things to say and said nothing. She went on quietly: 'If Mam had still been alive it'd have been different, I could have talked to her. I just couldn't talk to Dad, the way he was going on at me.'

Still Bawtry kept his thoughts to himself. He understood that she wanted to talk everything out, like a kind of therapy.

'Mam got killed in an accident while we were on holiday in the Lakes. She stepped into the road in front of a car, just like I did, only she got killed. I was fifteen, going to grammar school.'

Bawtry remembered the circumstances

55

now. Puberty was a bad time for a girl to lose her mother. It couldn't have been easy for her, probably impossible to talk about intimate things to her father. There was an aunt who came in and kept the house straight and did some of the shopping, but it wasn't like having a mother to confide in. And Raynes had never married again; even if he had it wouldn't necessarily have helped his girl. He had tried to be a good father, but trying wasn't enough; it depended on how you tried.

As if responding to his unspoken reflections, Alison Raynes said: 'I can see now that Dad was doing his best for me. Well, I dare say I always knew that, but it was the way he did it that put my back up. So I started going out at night, not telling him where I'd been, one row after another. It all seemed to get . . . oh, I don't know, sort of hopeless.'

'You haven't seen him today, I take it?'

'No, he came last night and he'll be back at visiting time today. It's funny, but I have a feeling now that we're going to get on better. Happen I should have an accident at regular intervals.' She smiled. 'No, that's not right. It's talking to you that's helped.'

'I'm glad,' said Bawtry.

'When I was a little girl I used to climb up his legs and then he'd swing me round and round. I thought he was the most wonderful man on earth.'

'Then you found out he was human with human faults.'

'I suppose there was something of that in it.'

'The relationship always seems to get difficult when you start to grow up. It changes again as you get older, for the better.'

'I can't imagine all this happening to you.'

'You mean you can't imagine me as a kid.'

She looked hard at him. 'Yes, I think I can. Even though you always seem — well, sure of yourself.'

'I'm not always sure, Alison. But one thing I do know for sure is that your Dad loves you.'

'Yes, I realised that last night. It was

just something in the way he sat here with me, never saying a word about all the trouble we've had. I think we're going to get on all right when he comes back today.'

Bawtry said: 'I haven't told him you were with Terry Byass.'

'I'm going to tell him myself, and about what you've done for me.'

The day sister drifted up and said: 'It's not really visiting time, inspector. You can have another minute or two, no more.'

Alison Raynes laughed. 'The great Inspector Bawtry being quietly told where he gets off. Would they take me on in the Force?'

'You're being serious?'

'I've been thinking about it since you came. Dad would be glad, wouldn't he?'

'Yes.' Bawtry smiled. 'Me, too, I think. If you really mean it, I'll see what can be done.'

'You haven't asked me a lot of questions about Terry,' she said unexpectedly.

'Why, should I have done?'

'I wondered at first if you'd just come

here trying to find out anything I might know about him. I'm glad you just came to see me.'

'I wasn't thinking about him, not in that sense. In any case, so far as I know he hasn't done anything illegal lately.'

'Suppose I know something?'

'Then, as a coming WPC., you have a duty to tell me. In fact, you have that duty simply as a private citizen.'

She shook her head. 'Actually, I don't know anything like that. I simply met him casually knocking about town. I just said I'd go for a run in his car, on impulse.'

'Where *were* you going?'

'Out into Cheshire for a meal. He said we'd finish up at his place, but I wasn't going to, you know.'

'You might have had trouble when you told him that,' answered Bawtry. A thought came to him and he added: 'What did he mean about his place? He lives in Santon Street with his old fella.'

'Then he must have moved. He said he had a place of his own, a house standing by itself in Burnside Grove, just off the West Derby Road, up near Sheil Park.'

'He must be up to something, having his own place and a car and money to chuck about,' said Bawtry with a grin. 'Perhaps I'd better look him up, after all.'

He took his leave and found the house. The garden was a jungle of grass and weeds and the house looked as if nobody lived in it. He tried the heavy brass knocker, but there were no answering footsteps. Maybe Terry Byass was just talking big. Or had gone out.

Either way, it would keep, thought Bawtry, and drove back to Headquarters.

5

Matt Lancing sat behind the walnut executive desk going through the books, not for the first time. The company was running a massive overdraft on its current account and even when foreign exchange came in for the latest export deal they'd still be in the red because operating costs, not least a wages bill that had to be met every week, didn't wait for overseas payments to arrive.

The company was in the machine tools business, selling steadily at home and with an expanding demand abroad. In fact, it was doing well — but if everything was squared-up a flock of questions would clamour for the answers he couldn't give, and the day of the independent audit was nearing.

It was two years since he got a fifty-one per cent hold on the business when the shares of old Julius Lancing, together with estate of £27,000 net, fell cosily into his lap. Mastering the ramifications of the company's affairs had posed no problem because he had once practised as a chartered accountant. Also, he had charm by the bucket-load. Within months he had won the confidence of the Board, so that he became the natural choice for managing director when the existing incumbent died at the seventeenth hole from a coronary. The chairmanship followed. All in all, a nice fat inheritance except for the fear — never wholly banished — that it might not last. That was why, for some time now, he had assumed direct personal charge of the company finances. In fact, he had embarked on a systematic sequence of fraudulent conversion and falsification of accounts, siphoning off mounting chunks of hard cash in a complex train of mythical transactions, covering-up with endless crooked entries. The resulting jigsaw would take auditors months to disentangle — if they ever found out, and the time was coming when they would. The bank was getting restive, there was no more collateral to throw in, and several shareholders were beginning to ask tentative questions. The first distant rumblings of the gathering storm.

Well, it didn't matter. In little more than twelve months he had bled the company white. By now he had a total of £275,000 salted away in seven numbered accounts in Swiss banks, all of it converted into selected currencies. He had his passport, made out in the name of Matthew Lancing, though the real Matthew Lancing was dead, very dead and buried under the floor of a hut in the squalor of Hong Kong's most densely crowded district — with Matthew Langley's passport in his pocket.

He thought back to the night they had met. In the North Star Bar it was. That was nearly two years to the day, and what a piece of luck, even to the extent that they had the same given names so that he hadn't had to adjust to being called Matt. He had drifted to the Far East from San Francisco and before that London and some points along the way: a smooth-talking con man on the run from one place to another as each became a little too hot. Like the time in St. Louis which had nearly ended in disaster after he had separated a visiting Texas cattleman from thirteen thousand dollars. He had got out in the nick of time, taking off for 'Frisco and then on to Hong Kong.

When he ran across Matt Lancing he was down to his last thousand bucks. Lancing was a drunk, not drinking to the point of total oblivion, a sort of controlled alcoholic. But on the sweltering night in the North Star he was hitting it harder than usual — 'Celebrating my good fortune, ol' boy. Join me, eh?'

At first Matt had scarcely listened. Just another lush talking a lot of cock. But after a little while the import of what the other was rambling on about riveted his attention. A letter from a firm of solicitors in Liverpool, a dead uncle leaving him an inheritance, fifty-one per cent of some bloody company or other. The boozy words swirled like a muddied stream, but now Matt was listening, fitting the disjointed confidences together, making a pattern. At the centre of it was the picture of money about to fall into the hands of a man who had been out of England since he was twenty, which was a quarter of a century ago, a man nobody who mattered had seen since he was young and couldn't identify.

'I'm the prodigal son about to enter into his inheritance,' Lancing had cackled. He grinned loosely. 'Prodigal nephew, to be correct. Good ol' Uncle Julius, thash what I say.'

Matt thought: some bastards have all the luck, wish it was me. Even as the stray reflection impinged on his mind, it started to grow. He looked across the table at his companion: about the same height and age, the same heavy jowls, though there was no direct facial resemblance. But that didn't matter, nobody in England had seen this fellow for twenty-five years.

I'm letting my imagination run away with me, Matt thought. But the idea stayed with him. Suppose he *did* turn up and claim the inheritance; who was going to say he was an imposter? You can't get away with it, chum. Why can't I? Matt bought another round and sat there listening to his thoughts and savouring the prickly excitement they fired within him.

Lancing put his new drink down in one and said: 'Lesh get a woman, eh — how about that?'

'They're easy to come by in this town,' Matt said indifferently.

'A beautiful Chinese girl, I've never had a Chinese girl.'

'No?'

'Thash right, I haven't. I once had a Turkish one.' His bloodshot eyes peered owlishly. 'In Cyprus, or was it Greece? Who cares?'

'Turkish delight, eh?'

Lancing crackled again. 'Thash right, Turkish delight. In a regimental brothel, officers only.'

'While you were in the Army?' Matt thought: if this twit was in the Army maybe a lot of fellows know him and can identify him.

'No, never in the Army, ol' boy. I met a chap in Cyprus or Crete or was it in Cairo?'

'Make your mind up,' said Matt.

The other waved an arm. 'Doesn't matter. I was having a drink somewhere and got friendly with this captain and he took me along with him.'

'You mean you never saw him again?'

'Never saw him again. Thash sad, isn't it? So awfully sad.'

Matt could hear himself breathing relief. 'And you've been on the trot from one place to another ever since?'

'Always on the move, a globe-trotting bum, thash me. Always broke. The times I used to think I wish I was a rich man.'

'Well, now you're going to be — unless you're merely inheriting some tuppenny-ha'penny company in hock to the bank.'

Lancing sat hugging his whisky glass in both hands. A knowing smile moved on his slack mouth. 'Thash where you're wrong, ol' boy. Ve-ry going concern. I've checked. *And* money left by my uncle, how much I haven't yet been told.'

'That's fine, then.' Matt spoke mechanically. The mad idea was expanding like a blown balloon. Only it wasn't mad, was it? All he had to do was present himself in Liverpool as Matthew Lancing and the jackpot was his for the taking. But it couldn't be as easy as that, there must be a snag somewhere. He'd find out, no hurry.

'When're you setting off for England?'

'Tomorrow, the noon flight.'

'London?'

The other nodded. 'Change planes there for Liverpool; only it's called something else, the airport I mean.'

'Speke.'

'So it is — speak to me only with thine eyes. The Chinese girl, I mean.'

'You've had too much booze, you'll never be able to do it.'

'Try me!'

'Alcohol stimulates the sexual urge while denying the means of its gratification.'

'Who says?'

'Lord Chesterfield I think.'

'You can tell him from me he's wrong.' Lancing peered round the smoke-hazed bar. 'A cute Chinese chick is what I want.'

'I know a good place,' said Matt carelessly. 'Safe, too.'

'You do? Why didn't you say so before?'

'How do you come to be out here?'

'Just drifting. Been here about a month. I was moving on, anyway. I picked up nearly six hundred quid playing the tables at the Horseshoe Club. I was going to the States.'

'And now you're off to dear old England.'

'White cliffs of Dover, here I come.'

'Or the Liver bird.'

'You know Liverpool?'

'I was there once, years ago.' In fact, Matt had stolen a cheque book from the inside pocket of a man who hung his coat up in the wash-room of the Adelphi Hotel. The cheques had the owner's name printed on them and he signed one for £400 in payment for a car which he promptly drove to Manchester and flogged to a dealer for £390. That was the only time he had been in Liverpool and he had never expected to see the place again. Until now.

Twenty minutes later he knew pretty well all there was to know about Matthew Lancing. The man was a ne'er-do-well, as anonymous as a toilet roll. The solicitor's letter had gone to his last known address, a flat off the Fulham Palace Road, and had been returned. Finally, they put an announcement in the Press and Lancing, an avid reader of newspapers, saw it nearly two weeks later. As simple as that.

Nobody in England had seen him in twenty-five years and if anyone even remembered him the image would be of a clean-cut young fellow, which he had long ceased to be.

Matt decided what he had to do. He pushed his wicker chair back and said: 'If you still want a bit of Chinese I'll take you to this place.'

They went out of the bar. Matt said: 'We can walk, it's not far.'

In fact, it was no more than a few hundred yards. They went down an alley and into a disused house, little more than a hut.

They were inside when Lancing hesitated. 'This isn't a . . . ' But he never finished the objection. The single blow behind his left ear felled him to the rickety floor. Matt closed the door and finished the job with strangling hands.

★   ★   ★

All this happened nearly two years ago and he had never had the smallest disquiet — until today.

6

It happened at four o'clock in the afternoon. The telephone rang and the girl on the office switchboard said: 'Call for you, Mr. Lancing.'

'Who is it?'

'A Mr. Leng, Mr. Thomas Leng.'

Matt said brusquely: 'Never heard of him. What does he want?'

'I don't know, sir, but he asked me to say he was from Hong Kong.'

Matt Lancing felt his hand go tight on the receiver. His whole body seemed to freeze. It was crazy, nobody could possibly know what he had done in Hong Kong. He had been in and out of the colony in less than twenty-four hours, had scarcely spoken to anyone except the real Matt Lancing. It was long ago, nearly two years ago, nobody could link him with anything; it was impossible, ridiculous. But someone was on the telephone, someone who had been in Hong Kong.

Christ, *have* I slipped-up somewhere?

Aloud, he said: 'It doesn't mean anything to me — but well, all right, put him through, will you?'

'Very good, sir.'

Then the voice was coming over the line. A middle-pitched voice with a vaguely sing-song quality. He had never heard it before in his life, he was certain.

'Hello, Matt — how's everything?'

For a moment he nearly panicked; an almost overmastering compulsion to slam the receiver down and flee possessed him, so that he couldn't even speak. You bloody fool, take a grip on yourself. Stall him off, say nothing; no, that won't wash, this fellow *knows* Matt Lancing, he *must* know him. Suppose he's found the body? No, that's not it or he wouldn't be ringing. I'll have to see him, I'll *have* to. But not now, not with the staff on the premises and the chance of being overheard. He forced calmness into his voice, trying to make it sound something like the voice of the man he had killed. 'Why, hello, this *is* a surprise.'

'Thought it would be. Didn't expect to

see me again, eh?'

'Well, no . . . '

'You sound different.' The caller's voice suddenly had a small edge to it. Or am I just getting jittery? I don't know. God Almighty, why did this have to happen?

Matt said: 'It's probably a bad line at your end. Also, I've got a cold.'

'Sorry about that. Look here, we must meet.'

'Sure. Where are you?'

'In a call-box at the Adelphi.'

The Adelphi; that brought back a memory. Well, whoever this bastard was he wasn't short of a bob or two. Or had he simply walked in and used a phone? What the hell did it matter?

'How about joining me over a drink — say at five-thirty?' the voice asked.

It was the last thing he was likely to do. Even as the thought disturbed him he saw a way out. 'I've a better idea. Why not come along here? I've a private bar with some special Scotch.'

'Sounds great.'

'I'll be tied-up until six. Suppose you drop in just after that?' The staff went home at five forty-five. The coast would be clear.

'Right, expect me then, on the dot. 'Bye now, Matt.'

He made a sound and hung up. His hands were wet with sweat, even his shirt was damp against the small of his back. He looked at the wall clock. Just under two hours to go. Two hours to figure out what he was going to do.

There was a tap on the door. Delaney, the export sales manager, came in. Something about guaranteed delivery dates to a customer in Hamburg. He could tell Delaney was going to make a big thing of it. Matt cut him short.

'I'll see Jamieson and impress on him that meeting the agreed date is a top priority.'

'That's fine, Mr. Lancing, only it'll be necessary to . . .'

'I said I'd see him. Now, if you'll excuse me.'

Delaney said obstinately: 'There are several points I must bring to your attention.'

'Bring them first thing in the morning.'

'But . . . '

'You heard, didn't you?' His voice was like a tormented nerve. Don't lose control, mate.

Delaney stared. His face, normally pale, had flushed.

Somehow, Matt got a smile out. 'I'm sorry, but I'm really up to the eyes in it just at the moment. Werner-Fath have been on the line, some problem I'll have to settle today.' It was a lie, the first thing that had come into his head, but it would serve. Anything would serve if it gave him time to think, time to work out what in heaven's name he was to do. 'Pop in first thing in the morning, I'll put everything else on one side. Right?'

Delaney nodded. He hesitated, seemed about to say something else but didn't. The door closed behind him.

Air gusted from Matt's dry mouth, a surge of relief. He picked up the receiver and told the girl on the switch not to put any more calls through, no matter from whom. That took care of the bloody phone. Then he remembered that his secretary was coming in for dictation.

There were seven letters, all important, due to catch the night mail. He tipped a key on an annunciator-box.

'Yes, Mr. Lancing?'

'Oh, Margaret — about those letters. They'll have to stand over till the morning. Something's cropped-up that'll keep me busy the rest of the day, or what's left of it.'

'I could stay on, if you wanted.' Even in his near-terror the thought came to him that Margaret Ayton was just about the best of secretaries.

'No, no, they're not *that* important. Tomorrow at ten. We'll get them done in time for the noon collection.'

'Just as you wish, Mr. Lancing.'

He got up from the desk and went behind the small curved bar spanning a corner of the wide room. He kept it for VIP callers and had never used it himself before. But now he needed a drink, badly. Better keep it to a drink singular, he was going to need a clear mind to handle this situation. But he had to have a drink, a stiff one to quieten the turmoil inside him. He poured the whisky and drank it in one. Small fires weaved through his bloodstream. He reached out again, then stopped himself. No more — don't be a fool, no more.

Time passed, interminably. He sat in his padded executive chair, trying to see the way out. This man Leng would know he was an imposter the instant they met. He had to be silenced. Perhaps money would buy him. Suppose it wouldn't — what then?

Matt's eyes swivelled again to the bar. He could play the perfect host, urbane and suave. 'My dear chap, I haven't a notion of what you're talking about — this fellow you knew out in Hong Kong must have been impersonating *me*!' The unruffled front, eh? Let's have a drink while we talk this absurd business out. A drink. Pity he couldn't make it a knockout drink, for good and all . . . *why not*?

He jumped half out of his seat, then sat back and slid open the top drawer of his desk and reached inside for the bottle of tablets he had bought in Hong Kong in case he had trouble sleeping after what he had done out there, but he had had no trouble. He looked at the tablets. How many made a fatal dose? He didn't know, but if you took enough of them in one go that would do it all right, especially if you'd been drinking previously. He recalled reading about an inquest on some fellow who took barbiturates after a night on the hard stuff; like a passport to eternity.

His breath came down his nose in a rustle. It was worth trying, more than worth trying. They would be alone in the office, nobody'd even see Leng arrive. It might work. It had *got* to work.

The clock hands showed five forty-seven. He went out into the main office. Empty. The staff had gone. Better make sure, though. He went from room to room. It was all right. Wait a minute, there's a light from old Fairfax's cubbyhole. He yanked the door fully open and there was Fairfax bent over a file. Pushing sixty-three and still over-conscientious.

Matt said amiably: 'Time you wcrc off, Fairfax.'

'I was just staying on to finish off

something, Mr. Lancing.'

'It can wait till morning.'

Fairfax blinked behind gold-rimmed spectacles. 'Another quarter of an hour'll see it out.'

'You've had a busy day. Now off you go.'

Fairfax looked uncertain.

'It's an order,' said Matt.

'Well, if you say so, Mr. Lancing.'

'I've just said it.' He tried to keep an edge out of his voice, not too successfully.

Fairfax tidied the filed papers, put them carefully in a marked folder, carried it to a shelf, changed his mind, carried it back to his desk and opened a deep drawer. For Christ's sake, why does he have to make a meal of it? Matt wanted to scream the words, but somehow he managed to stand there with a bland smile. He stretched his left hand, looking at the gold watch on his wrist. Five fifty-six. Four minutes to go, perhaps a few more. Sweat started down his back again.

Fairfax picked up his raincoat, put his hat on and said: 'Well, goodnight then, Mr. Lancing.'

'Goodnight, Fairfax.' He organised a smile to go with the words. 'I'll lock up after you, then I'm off myself.'

Fairfax took the back stairs. He always went that way because there was a short cut from the rear to his bus stop. Matt could hear him going down the winding stone steps. The relief was like something tangible.

He strolled back into his office and sat behind the desk, composing himself. Minutes passed. The commissionaire rang through to say would it be all right for him to leave and would Mr. Lancing be sure to lock the front entrance doors. Yes, of course, yes. And now he was alone in the entire place, waiting. Not for long. There was a distant whirring as the lift came up, then new footsteps and a tap on the door.

'Come in.'

The door opened and he was seeing Leng. Late thirties, dark hair, almost blue-black and a long face with a light tan, or was it a faintly Oriental pigmentation? Hard to say. Not Chinese, though. The eyes were pale blue, heavily lidded and alert. Matt thought: I'll not fool this one. But, suddenly, his nerves had stopped jumping. He was going to handle this, he'd *got* to handle it.

Leng walked slowly across the floor, splayed both hands on the desk and said: 'You're not Matt Lancing.'

Matt waved a ringed hand. 'Take a seat, Mr. Leng, while you explain that extraordinary statement.'

'There's nothing to explain except that I know Matt Lancing and you're not him.' Leng sat down, hitching up the trousers of his navy blue suit.

'You mean you know someone who claimed to be Matt Lancing.'

The long face smiled thinly. 'Don't try that on me, Mister Whoever-You-Are.'

Matt sat back, tipping his fingers like a pyramid. 'I'm under the impression that *you're* trying something, my friend.'

'Look,' said Leng, 'I palled out with Matt Lancing in Hong Kong.'

'You palled out with a man who told you that was his name.'

Leng laughed. He had a curious way of

doing it, his long mouth remaining shut while one side of it curved downwards. 'It'll not work, you know. Might have done but for one thing. Want to know what it is?'

'You're going to tell me, anyway, aren't you?'

'That's right, I'm going to tell you. Matt Lancing inherited this business.'

'Well, well! That's hardly news, is it?'

'Don't give me that line!' Leng snarled.

'I'm not giving you any line, my friend. I'm still waiting to hear what you mistakenly regard as proof of your absurd accusation concerning myself. Meanwhile, has it occurred to you that I can pick up the telephone and fetch the police here?'

Leng's eyes glittered. 'Go ahead, I'm not stopping you.'

Matt reached out a hand, then withdrew it. 'I'll hear you out first, I think.'

'I thought you might.' Leng's gaze ranged round the handsomely-appointed room, finally staying on the bar. 'Do yourself well, don't you?'

'You'll be asking me to offer you a drink next.'

'Why not? I could use one.'

Matt forced the triumph out of his voice. 'Your recent manner hardly suggests that we're likely to become drinking companions. Where did you meet this man who claims to be me?'

'I told you. In Hong Kong — as if you didn't know, anyway.'

'And he actually claimed that he had inherited this business?'

For a second Leng's face was less than fully confident. Matt thought: it's going to be all right, this bastard doesn't really know — just stumbled on something, that's all.

Leng lit a cigarette, blew the match flame out and said: 'I'll be straight with you. I met Lancing over some drinks and we got matey. He told me he was expecting a bit of good news and we arranged to meet in a few days. He never showed up.'

'So he didn't tell you anything specific!'

'That's right, he didn't. But that's not all. When he never showed up I thought nothing of it. He was just a drunk and I thought what the hell, I'll be seeing him some time. Only I didn't. In fact, I never set eyes on him again.'

Matt lifted a hand in order not to hide a yawn.

Leng leaned forward. 'But a month ago I was looking at a two weeks' old English newspaper and read a piece in the City column about this firm and the expansion plans of its chairman, Mr. Matthew Lancing.'

Matt remembered it. A couple of paragraphs, based on a telephone interview he had given at the paper's request. It had seemed a good idea at the time; a nice optimistic piece filling the shareholders with confidence. The possibility that it might be dangerous had never so much as occurred to him — why should it? But it was the small unconsidered things that sometimes exploded in your damned face. This had.

He was aware that Leng was speaking again. 'I thought at first the name must be a coincidence. Then I ran into a fellow who said Lancing had mentioned that he was going back to England to take over a machine tools business. Even then it didn't seem to matter, one way or the other. But after a while I started thinking about Lancing and his good luck. In plain English, I thought perhaps he might give me a nice soft job, just for old times' sake. I was sick of Hong Kong anyway, so I got a plane back to dear old England.'

'And checked-in at the Adelphi?'

Leng made a sour laugh. 'I'm not that bloody well-off, mate. I just went in the American bar for a drink and used one of their phones. I've got a room over a shop in Pitt Street, if you want to know.'

'Not particularly.'

The long-faced man went on: 'I rang up and got put through to Mr. Matthew Lancing — only the minute you came on the blower I felt pretty sure you weren't him. Now I bloody know.'

'Proof,' said Matt. 'How about that?'

'I know Matt Lancing and you're not him.'

'That's not proof, my friend.'

'No, it isn't, but if I repeat all this loud

86

enough and often enough it's going to be awkward for you — assuming I'm right, and I know I'm right.'

Matt picked up a desk pen and turned it slowly in both hands. This bastard could prove nothing, nothing whatever. But if he went round talking out loud he'd start something all right. He *had* to be stopped, here and now.

'Well, what are you proposing to do, Mr. Leng?'

'I could identify the real Matt Lancing, for a start.'

'He's probably drunk himself to death by now, from what you've said about his habits.'

Leng grinned wolfishly. 'Somehow you got to know the details of his inheritance and jumped his claim. But for you to get away with it he would have to be out of the running, right out of it.'

'My dear chap, I hope you're not accusing me of doing away with him.'

'Not necessarily. He could have had a heart attack. Anything, the state he was in. On the other hand, you might've given him a push.'

'You have a beautiful imagination, Mr. Leng. What else are you imagining?'

'I came here hoping that Matt might give me a nice easy job. I'm thinking of something rather better now.'

'Money, of course?'

'Of course.'

'Blackmail's an ugly word, my friend.'

'I can think of an uglier one.' Leng's gaze strayed to the bar again.

'I think,' said Matt cosily, 'I think we'd better join each other in a drink after all.' He went to the bar and came back with two large ones. 'Now I'll be frank with you, Mr. Leng. I knew Matt Lancing out in the colony, met him over some drinks, the same as you. He told me about this business and that he was flying back home. Well, it didn't mean anything to me.'

Leng sank the Scotch. Matt poured another, even bigger.

'If it didn't mean anything to you, what're you doing here then?'

'I met him several times,' lied Matt. 'The last time he looked in pretty bad shape. I took him back to his place and he had a massive heart failure. Dropped dead as soon as we got there.'

'And?'

'I switched our papers and passports, including the photographs, and assumed his identity. When they buried him it was in my name.'

'Which is?'

'You do want to know rather a lot, don't you?'

Leng laughed harshly. 'I already knew before I phoned you, mate. A fella found dead in Hong Kong, just before I left, a fella identified from a passport as Matthew Langley. Only he had a ring on his left hand, a big gold ring with a green stone set in the middle . . . *Lancing had one.*'

Matt felt sweat icing down the small of his back. Christ — why didn't I take the ring off? Aloud, he said: 'Even if you repeat your story you'd be disbelieved, but let's say I prefer that you keep it to yourself. *How much do you want?*'

'Five hundred down and two hundred a month.'

'Well, well!'

'Also, I want taking on the payroll in some capacity.'

'You don't want to *work* for it, surely?'

'Not so's you'd notice. I just want to keep an eye on you, *Mister* Lancing.'

Matt made two more drinks, appearing to consider. He handed one to Leng and said slowly: 'I think it can be arranged.'

'It'd better be,' said Leng. His speech was thickening.

Matt finished his drink, which was ninety-nine per cent American dry. 'Another?'

'Sure, why not?'

'Perhaps you'd rather have some money first, eh?' Matt unlocked the wall safe and came back with £500 in fives, tens and some of the new twenties. Leng poked at them with hungry fingers.

'I'll put you down as overseas sales consultant with a special brief to explore trade potential in the Far East, how about that?'

'I said I wanted to keep an eye on you.'

'You won't need to travel personally, you'll do all the planning from here and then send out a rep. We'll drink to it, eh?'

'Great!' Leng had the money now, fanning notes between his fingers like a stage card juggler.

Matt went behind the bar and reached for the already poured glass on the lower shelf, the one with enough soluble barbiturates to kill off a platoon.

'When do I start, tomorrow?' asked Leng.

'Not so fast as that, old chap. Got to make it look right, not too sudden. I'll have a letter sent off to you confirming that you're appointed to this new post.'

'No tricksh, mind.'

'No tricksh. Well, down the hatch with this one, shall we?'

The charged drink disappeared. Matt wondered if it had any kind of alien taste. Not that it mattered now. Besides, Leng was already more than half-cut and wouldn't notice, anyway. Well, it was done. How long before the stuff worked? He didn't know and wasn't waiting to find out. It was a piece of luck that his offices were no more than seven or eight minutes from Pitt Street — Leng ought to be able to walk that far before he collapsed. As long as it didn't happen on the office doorstep, thought Matt.

'You'd better put all that money in an envelope,' he said. 'I'll get you a large one.'

'All right.'

Matt brought an envelope. 'I'll show you a short cut out, Leng.'

'You do that.' Leng rose unsteadily. 'I'm loaded,' he said. A grin spread slowly across his face. 'Loaded with loot an' all.'

Matt cupped his elbow, steering him down the back stairs, the way Fairfax had gone. Better than going out the front way; no chance of being seen, not at this time. The stairs opened on a private parking site, used by the occupants of nearby offices. All gone now, not a car left.

They were on it when Matt thought there was a faint sound in the distance and stopped. Better hang back, just in case. 'You're a bit wobbly, we'll sit in my car for a few minutes,' he said.

He opened the rear door and Leng tumbled sideways on the seat. Matt listened acutely. Nothing. Don't get jumpy, mate. He delayed another minute, then said: 'You'll be all right now.' He helped Leng out. 'Straight down York Street and you're nearly home and dry.'

'You mean wet,' said Leng. He swayed slightly, but he could walk. Just about.

'A nice long sleep'll put you right,' said Matt. A very long sleep, the big sleep. He cradled an arm round Leng's shoulders, moving the other hand deftly.

Leng beamed meaninglessly and started down the short street. Matt stayed in the shadows, watching until the figure lurched out of sight. His breath came in gulps of relief. It was all right, everything was all right.

He walked up the stairs to his room and put the £500 he had taken off Leng back in the safe, locked up and went down for his car.

7

Another week of sultry Indian summer had passed since the Alison Raynes incident, with day temperatures soaring into the middle seventies; even at night the humid heat was overpowering.

'It's too bloody hot to work,' said George Lucas. He was a detective sergeant, about Bawtry's own age, less powerfully built but no less fit.

Bawtry grinned. 'It's too hot even for the villains. But they can't lay off for long. When their money runs out and they have to start tapping for a loan they'll be up to something. Some of them are probably at it this minute.'

Brooker loomed in the doorway, for once not preceded by a cheroot. He ran a finger round the inside of his shirt collar. 'Fancy a pint, you two?'

'I thought you never drank until you finished duty,' said Bawtry mildly.

'Well, that's a fact, I don't, but it's that

suffocating I'm making an exception. I could sink a pint shandy.'

'A shandy?' Lucas echoed the word in astonishment. It was as if Omar Khayam had called for lemonade.

'That's right, shandy with great chunks of ice in it, and happen a salmon and cucumber sandwich to go with . . . ' Brooker broke off as Fallon walked through from the courtyard. The Superintendent was wearing a blue suit he had had made for him less than a month previously, but somehow he still managed to convey the general aspect of an unmade bed. Privately, Ted Fallon envied Bawtry's suave dress sense, but had never been able to emulate it. He was a large shaggy man, already well past retiring age, with an over-long face which caused him to resemble a slightly saddened horse. He also owned as shrewd a brain as any in the Force.

Just at this moment the long face had a slight touch of animation and Bawtry noticed it. Fallon put an aged blackened briar between his teeth, mercifully not lighting it since he smoked the rankest brand of shag tobacco extant.

'Message just received by Information from Detective Constable Hollis,' he said. 'Man found dead in an entry off Pitt Street. Stabbed.'

Pitt Street was Chinatown, peaceful most of the time, better than in the old days. In fact, you could walk round the district more safely than in some of the new housing zones. Bawtry, who had pounded the Chinatown beat, as a green young copper in his first uniform, had kept in touch with the place; he liked the Chinese and they trusted him.

Fallon said, with a faint grin: 'The Terrible Three all together just at the right time. You'd better all get down there right away. I'll have the fingerprint and photo mob hard on your heels, also the vet.'

'Doc Magnus will simply love to hear himself described as a vet,' said Brooker, poker-faced.

'What he can't hear won't . . . ' It was Fallon's turn to break off. The small sound brought him round in a half-turn to see the police surgeon framed in the doorway.

'Taking the name of my noble profession in vain, shame on you, Ted,' grinned Magnus. 'All right — don't apologise. I just happened to look in, what's come up?' He listened, then said: 'I'll go in the squad car, save a bit of petrol that way.'

Car Five-Nine-Zero was in and re-routed. They went west down Hanover Street and on to the Chinese section — changed in recent years, like so much of the city. Hollis was on the pavement at the mouth of a dark entry.

'Know who the fella is?' This from Brooker.

'No, sir.'

'What — no papers, driving licence, anything?'

'Just a ballpoint pen, cigarettes, matches, some loose change, a wallet with twenty quid in it and an envelope stuffed with toilet paper, sir.'

'You're not joking, are you, Hollis?'

'No, sir.'

'*Toilet* paper. What the hell would anyone carry toilet paper about for?'

'Happen he was just taking precautions, sir.'

'Not funny.'

'No, sir.'

'Let's see him,' said Brooker tersely. He glanced up at the entry and made out the inscription: *Tiensen Alley*. 'You *did* find the body in this place, Hollis?'

'Yes, sir.' The detective constable looked puzzled.

'I was just thinking of the old story about the P.C. who dragged a dead horse from Cazneau Street into Fox Street because Cazneau was harder to spell.'

'Oh, I see. No, he hasn't been moved, not even a few inches.'

The dead man looked in his late thirties. He was lying on his back with his right leg drawn up under him. Very dark hair, not over-long, but not a short back-and-sides, either. Navy blue suit over a white nylon shirt, the shirt bloodied on the left side where he had been stabbed. The knife wasn't in him.

Magnus went down on one knee. He was there for what seemed rather a long time. When he straightened up he said evenly: 'Do any of you know how long the body has been here?'

Hollis said: 'No, sir.'

'What makes you ask, doctor?' said Bawtry.

'This man has been dead about two hours, inspector.'

'Fatally stabbed and nobody saw the body . . . '

'He was stabbed, yes.' Magnus seemed to be speaking half to himself.

'You omitted the word fatal,' said Bawtry quietly.

'He didn't die from the stab wound,' replied Magnus.

Brooker stared. 'Dammit, he *must* have,' He came closer, sniffing. 'This fella reeks of whisky.'

'Yes, he does. It looks as if someone stabbed him, probably meaning to rob him, thinking he was drunk.'

'And not a fatal wound?'

'No, it didn't penetrate enough, or anything like it.'

'Do you mean he had a thrombosis or something, doc?'

The police surgeon hesitated, then said:

'It's possible this man had mixed drink and drugs. I'll have to find out.'

'How long will it take to establish the facts?'

Magnus shrugged. 'We'll have to get the toxicologist. It'll take some time. A day or more — longer in some cases. You know the procedure.'

'In broad terms, yes,' answered Brooker. 'Four main divisions of poisons and the chemist classifies them on the basis of physiological action, doesn't he?'

Magnus nodded. 'The volatile poisons are separated by distillation. The non-volatile ones, and these take in the new synthetic drugs, are separated from the tissue by solvents — the metallic ones by oxidation. That leaves matter like oxalic acid which can't be separated by the other techniques.'

'You're putting me off my food, doc.,' said Brooker, wryfaced.

'All this is only the initial process,' Magnus added.

'It means waiting,' Brooker growled. 'What do we do meanwhile?'

'That's up to you fellows.' Magnus

smiled thinly. 'But I'm willing to put my neck out enough to suggest that you work on the assumption that this man was already dying when he was stabbed and that death may be due to a combination of drink and drugs.'

Bawtry, who had been listening in silence, said: 'Could the drugs be barbiturates?'

'Well, that does happen. I don't know yet, though. Why?'

'Just that a man wouldn't ordinarily take them outside the privacy of his own home,' replied Bawtry.

Brooker almost jumped. 'You mean somebody poisoned this fella and then stabbed him and dumped him here to throw us off the scent?'

'I'm merely considering possibilities, no more than that. But no less.'

'Christ,' said Brooker. 'Now we've got a bent bastard on our hands.'

'*When* we find him,' rejoined Bawtry drily.

'Damn it, Sam, we've *got* to find him,' exploded Brooker. 'We'll go through the entire area with a tooth-comb.'

Police cars swung into the street. The old routine began — chalk marks and measuring tape, graphite dusting, flashing camera lights, finally the ambulance crew taking the body away.

Brooker got through to Information, calling for more C.I.D. men. The area was cordoned off, all traffic stopped, every resident in the street to be questioned, detailed statements taken and signed.

'We'll probably get nowt, but we have to try,' Brooker rumbled. 'There's always the chance that somebody saw *something*.'

'Li Chou has a house near here,' mused Bawtry. 'I'd like to chat him up.'

'Well, you might get more out of him than the rest of us, you being a friend of his. All right, then.'

Bawtry nodded and went down the street, turning off it. The house was in a square that was scarcely more than a wide yard, between Gilbert Street and Lydia Ann Street. A gaunt three-storey house crouched behind flaked iron railings. Age-worn stone steps led up to a massive pitted door with a faded stained-glass inset. The door was on the latch, not locked. Li Chou never locked his house; nobody in the district would even contemplate stealing from him.

The door moved against the pressure of Bawtry's palm, opening on a bare hall with olive green walls and cracked linoleum whose pattern had long since vanished. Bawtry was about to call out when his notrils caught the drifting incense in air already heavy with the aftermath of cooked rice. It was coming from a room on his right. He opened the door and stood framed in the opening. A dozen men were lying on rugs and cushions, drawing in turn on a long-stemmed bamboo pipe. Li Chou was not among them. The scent was strong now, the sickly scent of opium. The men didn't see him, they were far off in the small private world where the aches of body and mind had ceased and the quiet torment of living was mercifully stilled. None of the men were less than middle-aged.

Bawtry knew he would have to book them, but not yet. If you took an opium smoker from his pipe before he had finished the agony would be almost beyond endurance. He closed the door and walked on down the hall. At the far end another door opened on a wide living-room.

Li Chou was seated at the table with an open book. Without looking up he said gently: 'Please to enter, Mr. B.'

'I thought you'd seen me, Li.'

'Just a small glance as you arrive.' The crinkled mouth of a face aged like yellowed parchment made an almost imperceptible movement. 'Always you are welcome in the House of the Gilded Dragon, though Li wish you had chosen another time.'

'Because of the smokers?'

Li Chou inclined his head, skull-capped with wisps of hair struggling outwards like wild strands of greying straw.

'I didn't know you let a room off for smoking,' Bawtry said.

'It is not my custom, Mr. B. But the place where they smoke after rice time is not available, so for once I break my rule.'

'You're also breaking the law, you know that.'

'I lament the necessity, but they are old and honoured friends, old in years too. The young Chinese no longer smoke the pipe, so it cannot be said that Li Chou leads them into what you would call the bad ways.'

'Do you know who the pusher is?'

'I do not ask my guests such a question,' murmured Li Chou reprovingly.

'Just the same, you know.'

Li Chou smiled, a long slow smile full of nothing. Bawtry knew it would be a waste of time to probe. Nobody in the house was going to tell him that; to do so would be to cut off their supplies.

'Please do not arrest my guests until they have finished their pipes,' Li said.

'You don't have to ask that.'

Li bowed. 'You are a good man, Mr. B. Later, when the opium is no more than dross in the slot of the pipe, they will go with you to the House of the Police.' The old Cantonese sighed. 'It is unfortunate that you observe my good friends.'

Bawtry didn't answer immediately. He knew well enough what he ought to do, but finally he said: 'I don't believe I have seen your good friends, Li.'

The eyes under the crumpled lids showed nothing. 'I am grateful, Mr. B. Always my friends have smoked the pipe, but they do no harm to others.'

Bawtry grinned to himself. The Chief Con would tear a strip off him if he knew; on the other hand, perhaps not.

'You do not visit my house because of the smoking, then?' Li Chou's slightly high voice carried a new note, a rising interrogation.

'No, a man has just been found stabbed only a short distance from here, in an entry off Pitt Street.'

'He is dead, this unfortunate person?'

'Yes.' Bawtry decided not to disclose that the stab wound wasn't fatal; not yet, anyway. The less anyone outside the Force knew the better. Instead, he went on: 'If he has been living near here you will know him. No man so much as moves in the Chinese quarter without your knowledge, Li.'

'You speak with the persuasive tongue of flattery, Mr. B.'

'I think you know me better than that. Will you come — now?'

'Your lightest wish is my imperative command,' intoned Li Chou.

They walked down the hall, not looking at the door behind which ageing men were living for a little while in a paradise whose celestial peace dissolved all past regrets and future fears. Ten minutes later they were going into the dark sprawling building which had been an asylum for the blind before it became the Head-quarters of the Liverpool and Bootle Constabulary. Bawtry remembered that some jokers on the strength liked to say it still was an asylum. Happen it was at times, though to men whose working lives were centred on it the place was virtually an extension of their beings.

The body was on a slab. A white-overalled attendant pulled the sheet back. Li Chou stood looking down. Then he said simply: 'This man is Tom Lcng.'

'Sounds Oriental, but apart from the blue-black hair he doesn't look Chinese, not full Chinese.'

'His grandfather was from China, his grandmother from England. Tom Leng's father also married an English girl. So the Chinese strain is but partial.'

'Where's he been living?'

'He took a room above the shop occupied by Kai Wah in Pitt Street. This was but recently, when he arrived from Hong Kong.'

'Seeking work here, you mean?'

'Not work. He come because he wish to seek someone. A man called Langley. I do not know such a one.' There was a small inflexion in Li Chou's voice, almost imperceptible, but Bawtry noticed it.

'You don't know but you have thoughts, old friend.'

Li Chou smiled. 'There is nothing you miss, Mr. B. But my thoughts are not, as you would say, evidence.'

'I'd like to hear them, Li. They may have some bearing on the case. This man has been murdered.'

They went into the interview room. A uniformed constable brought two beakers of tea. Li Chou shook his head. Well, it wasn't the kind of tea he was accustomed to.

'Now then,' said Bawtry.

'It is but little. Tom Leng does not tell me anything, but I sense that he is seeking this man with a purpose.'

'What purpose?'

'Perhaps to right a wrong. I cannot be sure, but I think this from the way he speak to me. I am sensitive to such things. But I may be wrong.'

'A man named Tom Leng comes all the way from Hong Kong looking for a fella and somebody stabs him almost outside the place where he has taken a room.' Absently, Bawtry picked up his tea without sipping it. 'He didn't ask you to help him find this man?'

'I think he knew where to look.' Li Chou passed a veined hand over his skull cap. 'He say one thing, though — he expected their meeting to be a good thing for him, personally.'

'That could mean money, perhaps blackmail.'

Li Chou shrugged. 'Who can say?'

'What sort of man was Leng — a good man?'

'I think perhaps not.'

'A villain?'

'I do not know that, Mr. B — he arrive but recently.'

'Why did he come to you?'

'He did not come to me. I took the opportunity to speak with him. Always it is my way to meet all who come to live in this area.'

'You just chatted him up and formed the opinion that he was after this fella for some purpose, possibly having to do with money?'

'That is so.'

'I'd better find this man, then.' Bawtry grinned wryly. 'A fella with a fairly common name but no known habitation. There's probably a few Langleys on Merseyside, but none of them may be this one.'

'You will still find him, Mr. B.,' said Li Chou in parting.

'I wish I was as sure.'

Bawtry went out into the main office and Joe Oldfield said: 'They've got a suspect for the stabbing, Sam . . .'

8

Bawtry stopped as if someone had banged a door in his face. 'What, already?'

'That's right, they're bringing him in. Be here in a minute.'

'Who've they booked?'

'Some young fella. Hollis found him in a coffee bar with a knife. Stains on the blade and he couldn't account for his movements at the relative time.'

Oldfield looked sideways as the detective constable came in with a boy handcuffed to him, followed by two uniformed branch constables. 'He wouldn't come quietly,' Hollis said. He looked at Bawtry. 'Do you want to take over, sir?'

'He's your prisoner, Hollis. Are you charging him?'

'Yes, sir. Being in unlawful possession of an offensive weapon, to wit a knife.' The detective constable went on, straight-faced: 'He says his name is Ho-Chi-Minh.'

The boy said:: 'I was just being funny. I hate pigs and I was just being funny, see?'

'We can find out your real name, you know that,' said Bawtry.

'You don't need to bother, it's Les Culley.'

'Address,' said Hollis.

'Ten Acorn Terrace, Everton.'

Bawtry said: 'Better formally charge him and take a statement.'

'Yes, sir.' Hollis hesitated. 'I'd sooner you did the interrogation, Mr. B.'

'Put him in the interview room and I'll join you in a few minutes, then.'

Culley spat on the floor. 'I got nowt to say to lousy pigs.'

'Book him,' said Bawtry.

Hollis took the youth away. Oldfield said heavily: 'This business of calling us pigs and fuzz, it's growing.'

'Only among a certain element, Joe.'

Oldfield rubbed his chin with a knuckle. 'We've always had enemies, that I know, but things were better in t'old days. Villains were villains and we knew where to find them. Now we're getting this hate from fellas like this one.'

'It's still a minority cult, Joe.'

'I hope you're right. This young fella — he's little more'n a boy. Going around with a knife, and blood on it.'

'We'll have the lab look at the stains. If they match up with those of the dead man it'll go badly for him.' Bawtry stayed on chatting for a short while, then walked into the nearly bare room where the interviewing was done. Culley was sitting, defiant-faced, at the plain desk. Hollis stood up and Bawtry took his place.

'No statement?'

'He refuses to say anything, sir.'

Bawtry pushed a twenty packet of Players across the table and said: 'We're informing your parents that you are here, Culley.'

The boy sneered. 'You don't need.'

'We're doing it, just the same.'

'You can keep my old fella out of it. All I'll get from him is a lot of I-told-you-so.'

'Where do you work?'

'I'm on t'dole.'

'How old are you?'

'Seventeen.'

'Have you had a job?'

'I've had half a dozen. What's it to you?'

'I just like to know things. Can't you keep a job?' Culley shrugged. His eyes focused on the cigarette packet.

'Have one, if you want,' said Bawtry.

'I've run out.' Culley dipped stained fingers into the packet and put a cigarette in his thin mouth. Bawtry's lighter flared.

'So you're not going to tell us why you were in possession of this knife?'

'You can get stuffed.'

'I don't know a good taxidermist.' Bawtry thought: I've said that before somewhere.

Culley blinked. 'Don't know what you're on about.'

'Doesn't matter. Where were you between the hours of seven-thirty and nine-thirty tonight?'

'In t'coffee bar listening to a pop group, records I mean.'

Hollis said evenly: 'Constable 497 James saw the owner of the coffee bar, William Arkwright. He says the accused was there at seven forty-five, went out and came back at eight-twenty.'

'Bloody liar,' said Culley.

Bawtry lit a cigarette himself. He seemed to be meditating. After a few moments Culley yelled: 'Well, get on with it, then.'

'What sort of work do you do, when you're working that is?'

'Labouring, on't one of the building sites.'

'Which one?'

'Several.'

'Why did you lose half a dozen jobs?'

'What's it to you?'

'Why?'

'I got fed-up, see?'

'No.'

'I went missing, then. Will that do?'

'Persistent absenteeism?'

'Call it what the hell you like. I got fed-up. They gave me my cards.'

'Is your old fella in regular work?'

'Yeh. So what?'

'He's better at holding a job down than you. Ever heard of a fella called Tom Leng?'

'Who's he when he's at home?'

'I just told you who he is. He lives over a little shop in Pitt Street.'

'I don't know no Chinese shops . . . ' Culley stopped, warily.

'I didn't say it was a Chinese shop.'

'What's the difference, they're all Chinks round there, aren't they?'

'Not all, these days. And you don't know Tom Leng?'

Les Culley said, not taking Bawtry's direct gaze: 'Never heard of him.'

'You probably never did, but you might know him, in a manner of speaking.'

Culley dragged on his cigarette, not speaking. His eyes were still avoiding Bawtry's.

'If you never heard of this man you won't be bothered that he's dead, then,' said Bawtry evenly.

The smouldering cigarette hung from Culley's mouth, stuck on his lower lip. 'Dead . . . ' He swallowed.

'That's right.'

'I never killed him.' Culley's voice was a croak.

'Who said you killed him?'

Culley rolled the cigarette free, wincing. 'You're trying to trap me, you bugger.'

'Somebody stabbed Tom Leng, probably between half-seven and eight. His blood will be on the knife.'

'I didn't . . . '

'I haven't said it's on your knife, Culley. But it'll be easy enough to find out, won't it?'

Culley broke out in the shivers. 'I din't kill him, I never meant to kill him. I was only just . . . '

'Only just what?'

The boy tugged at the fringed lapels of his imitation Western jacket. 'I seen a fella going down an entry in Pitt Street. He was reeling, like he was drunk. I give him a bit of a nick with the knife, just a nick it was, that's all.'

'You didn't even know this man, but you put the knife in him?'

'I was skint and I thought he's a drunk and won't know me again. I just prodded him with the knife and rolled him for his wallet. I din't even get it. I thought I heard someone coming and I beat it.'

Culley tongued dry lips. 'Christ — what've I done?'

'You attacked a man with a knife. Unlawful wounding. Object, larceny from the person. Robbery with violence.'

'I tell you I din't set out to kill him.'

Bawtry said impassively: 'You didn't.'

'Din't what?'

'Kill this man.'

'What!' Culley's eyes bulged.

'You wounded him, a minor injury. He was already dying when you did it and finally died, from another cause.'

Culley screeched: 'You stinking fuzz, you trapped me into saying what I did.'

'Happen I helped you along just a bit, but we'd have found out anyway if his blood's on your knife.' Bawtry stood up. 'For the moment you're charged with being in possession of an offensive weapon. If the bloodstains match up there'll be a more serious charge.'

He went out to his car. He was due off in less than an hour and he could have hung about Headquarters or even given himself an early cut, it would have been all right. Instead, he drove out to Terry

118

Byass's new place. It was still deserted. He was on the point of leaving when an old woman came along the street and said: 'You'll not find anyone in, she's gone off to stay with her sister in Chester.'

'Who has?'

'Millie Jenkins, what lives in t'house you're knocking on, young man.'

'I thought a young chap lived here.'

'Aye, he does, temporary that is. Some nephew or other. He told me Millie let t'house to him for t'duration like. While she's away.'

'Well, he doesn't seem to be in.'

'He comes in late mostly. I don't like him.'

'The feeling is mutual, ma'am,' said Bawtry. He tipped his hat and got back in the MG.

9

Della Lancing had stopped seeing Charles Bamer. Not because she any longer cared what Matt thought. She had defused that hazard all right; she had been a fool ever to worry about what Matt would do because he couldn't do anything, she had made sure of that.

They had first met on the plane from Heathrow to Speke. She was then thirty-two to Matt's forty-three. On her way to a new post, personal secretary to the head of a shipping firm with offices near Canning Place. They were instantly attracted, though both were experienced and wary of emotional involvement. But a month later they were married. It had taken Della less than that to decide that it was a mistake.

Matt was wealthy, established; he gave her an expensive home, her own car, a credit account at the best stores and no questions, everything she wanted. In return she gave him smiling affection, a meticulously-run domestic background, interest in his work. He had everything from her except one thing and that, almost before the honeymoon was over, she could no longer give eagerly. She had tried; God, how she had tried, but it was no use. In the end she was simulating a desire she had almost totally ceased to feel. If he was aware of it he gave no sign; but, then, he had never seemed demanding. Matt's real driving force was money; that and the sense of power which the possession of it conferred. But he cared about her, she knew that. It showed in a dozen ways, not least in the fact of his jealousy. That was why she had been afraid when she found him unexpectedly at home the night of that bloody car accident.

But there had been no need for fear because she had found out what he was up to. In fact, she still had no inkling of the complete truth about the man she had married; but she had guessed, accurately, that he was putting large sums of the company's money away in numbered accounts and he hadn't denied it. The knowledge had startled her, but it had nothing to do with her growing disenchantment about her marriage. The realisation of its underlying cause had been almost shattering, but now she faced it with a sort of cynical detachment: she wanted sex, but not from her husband.

This was not because she was attracted to the idea of permissiveness; in fact, she had a contempt for the whole contemporary trend. The kids — or, more accurately, some of them — seemed to treat the sexual relationship with about as much regard as blowing their noses. Everything made easy, matter-of-fact, taken for granted. Well, that wasn't how she looked at it.

The realisation of her own attitude came casually in a teatime chat with Connie Enders. Connie was pushing forty-six, a big blonde woman with a husband and three children, two of them in their late teens.

'I've brought them up right,' she said. 'No liberal-permissive ideas in *our* house.'

Della laughed. 'Well, I can't claim any

knowledge about what to tell one's children.'

'It's not so much what you tell them as the atmosphere of the home. Julie's seventeen but she has to be in by nine-thirty. No boys taking her out at night in their father's car, all that sort of bloody nonsense.' Connie lit a cigarette and blew the match flame out. 'The French have the right approach — put two young people of opposite sexes together, alone, and you're asking for trouble in a loud voice.'

'I thought the youngsters picked up permissive ideas anyway — at school and university.'

'Well, you can't put them in a cage, that's a fact. But the example of the home still counts, never mind what the so-called intellectuals yap at you these days. Also, I've taken care that my kids know a few of the basic realities of life.'

'I hope you've been successful, then.'

'You can't guarantee it, Della — but you can minimise the dangers.'

Della looked at her, this splendidly-constructed, amiable woman, all simple extrovert commonsense from the ten guinea shoes to the expensively-contrived casualness of her hair. 'You don't always live up to the highest moral principles yourself, do you?' she ventured.

'I have one or two boy friends, yes.' Connie made one of her booming laughs. 'Relieves the monotony of married bliss.'

'Aren't you ever scared stiff that George will get to know?'

'A little. Not so much as the boy friends. They're married and there's nothing so abjectly craven as an erring husband when he's just had his illicit oats.'

'I simply love the way you put it, Connie.'

'I believe in calling a spade a bloody shovel, darling. I'll tell you what it is. I like a little flutter on the side, just occasionally, but I absolutely hate all this permissive promiscuity. In fact, I don't like the way the damned world's going. I believe in all the despised Victorian-Edwardian virtues, right up to the hilt.'

'I thought some of our respectable ancestors stepped out of line, especially the men. Lip service to high moral traditions while popping round the corner to do what they shouldn't.'

'Of course, but that's not the point, is it?'

'I don't know. What is?'

Connie stubbed out her cigarette, turning it round and round in a heavy crystal tray. 'I think it's quite simple. Our fathers and grandfathers may have stepped out of line now and then, but they accepted the rightness of a moral code and ordered most of their lives by it.'

'The young call that hypocrisy.'

'I don't give a damn what they call it. The point is that it worked. At least people knew when they were sinning. They didn't call black white and *vice versa*. And having moral values, even if you fell by the wayside now and again, was a sight better than what we have now — public pornography, legalised abortion and homosexuality, kids getting in and out of bed with as much concern as getting in and out of their baths, if some of them take baths.'

'You're a very, very naughty girl, Connie.'

'No, I'm not. Just occasionally.' Connie Enders chuckled plumily. 'I'll tell you summat for nowt, as they say — sex was a damned sight more intriguing when it was a sin.'

Della said meditatively: 'I've never thought of it in that way.'

'You start thinking about it, darling. It might give you an idea or two when you're all alone by the telly while Matt's off on one of his business trips.'

She had thought of it all right. Not continually, but what Connie had said kept coming back to her, finally making a psychological answer to her emotional failures with Matt. Then she had met Phil Edgeley in that restaurant. It had gone on from there. And tonight Eddie Freeman was coming to the house. That was a risk she had never taken before, but this time she knew Matt was away — in Paris, not coming back until tomorrow, definitely. He had rung her up earlier, before lunch. A call for you from Paris, the overseas operator had said. No possibility of a slip-up this time. She had just put the receiver down when Eddie telephoned and on an impulse she had told him he could come to the house. A tremor possessed her briefly. *Not* in the marriage bed, I can't do that. In the spare room; that was all right, somehow almost respectable. Well, not quite that, but you know what I mean.

In fact, Matt had flown back from Orly late that afternoon. The business he had been negotiating had been finalised sooner than he anticipated. He had meant to ring Della when he got to the office, not because they were any longer eager to see one another, just to let her know he was here because if he caught her out again he would be forced to turn a blind eye and he couldn't trust himself to do it. Better not to know. Not yet, anyway. But something had come up at the office and he hadn't called his home. It was not until he was driving there that he remembered.

Eddie Freeman arrived at six-thirty. He was a merchant ship's captain from Tyneside, thirty-five years old, married with three children and not given to extra-marital adventures. He had literally bumped into Della while she was out shopping and one thing had led to another until each was aware of what the proximity of the other was doing.

And now here he was, in a taxi because he was on shore leave far from home and had no car. He paid the taxi off at the end of the road, walking the rest of the way and letting himself in at the back; she didn't want the neighbours to notice anything.

'Hi, Della!' he called softly.

'Why, Eddie, how lovely to see you.'

She came towards him and he took her in his arms. 'God, you're gorgeous.' He buried his face in her neck.

Della freed herself, laughing. 'Don't be so eager. We'll have a little drink, shall we?'

They had two drinks, not little ones. He was talkative in a slightly jerky, nervous way, and she noticed it.

'It's all right, darling,' she said calmly. 'My husband's in Paris.'

'Oh, I didn't realise he was abroad.'

The relief in his voice was like something tangible.

'That's right. My better half's in Paris and yours is in Newcastle and we're all alone and not feeling blue.'

He wished she hadn't said that. He didn't want to think about Ann and the children. What a shit he was. But he knew he was going to do it. A bird in every port, that's what they said about seafaring men, but it wasn't true of all of them and it hadn't been true about him, until now. But the woman lazing on the massive settee was different, her mere presence inflamed his senses. He wondered where it was going to be. Not on the settee, he decided. Christ, they weren't going to use the bed she shared with her husband, surely?

Without meaning to, he heard himself saying it.

She laughed. 'There's a nice warm cosy room right next to it. Then we'll go out on the town.'

He got up and sat alongside her. 'I can't believe it . . . '

She smiled, a long slow smile. He slid a

129

hand along her thighs, under her skirt. She wasn't wearing tights.

Della pushed the hand away and walked ahead of him. He followed, stripping off his jacket. The door made a small click behind them.

★ ★ ★

Bert Collins was cruising the police Zodiac down the wide avenue when his lights picked out a man running madly out of a side road. A tall rugged-looking fella carrying his shoes, shirt and jacket.

He ran straight out into the road. The police driver crashbraked, thrust his head through the wound-down window and yelled: 'What the hell . . . why, if it's not Eddie Freeman!'

Eddie panted: 'For God's sake, give me a lift, will you?'

Bert Collins swung the nearside door open. Eddie went round to it and nearly fell inside. 'Start driving, Bert — like the bloody clappers.'

They were going west down Walton

Hall Avenue when Collins said face-tiously: 'What the hell have *you* been up to? Not burgling a house, I hope.'

'Give over, you know me better than that.'

'If I didn't know you I'd be running you in.' Collins grinned. 'You weren't having crumpet and the husband unexpectedly turned up, were you?'

Eddie started. 'How did you know . . . ?'

'I didn't, I was joking. So *that's* it, is it?'

'I got to know a smashing piece and she invited me up to her house, said her old fella was away on business, in Paris.'

'Only he wasn't?'

'All I know is we were in the middle of it when a car came up the drive and I had to grab my clothes and beat it.'

'Lucky you ran into me, then. If it'd been a police driver who didn't know you he'd have marched you back to the place.'

Eddie shivered.

'Well, let it be a lesson to you,' said Bert Collins. 'And don't go round talking about it. Remember the old saying — if you had it last night just smile.'

Eddie looked up from putting his shoes on. 'If you want to know, I feel several sorts of a bastard.'

'Remorse gnawing at you, eh? It'll pass.'

'Not with me it won't. I don't like thinking about it.'

'Don't, then. You can't change it, so just forget it.'

They were near the bottom of Kirkdale Road making for the city centre when Bert Collins said: 'What's up now? You haven't spoken in minutes.'

'I'm bothered about something.'

'You got away without being seen, didn't you?'

'It's not that, it's something I happened to notice when I was going through the lounge on the way out. I didn't see it before because I was turned from it.'

'What?'

'A framed picture stuck on sort of a shelf, a photo it was. I only caught a glimpse, but it was enough.'

'What do you mean, a photo — a picture of her old fella?'

'It couldn't be. It was someone I met in

132

a bar, out in Hong Kong. A fella named Langley. We had a bit of a chat.'

'What of it?'

'I don't know, except that it seemed funny they had a picture of him.'

'Someone they just happened to know. Might be a relative.'

'I suppose so, only I can't get over seeing him there.'

'As long as you didn't see her husband, in the flesh!' Eddie Freeman let out a long breath. 'Yes — never again.' Bert laughed. '*That's* been said before.'

'It'll be true for me, Bert — the first time *and* the last.'

'You stick to that,' the driver said. 'Where d'you want dropping off? And it'll have to be on me route.'

'Anywhere near Lime Street'll do. And thanks a lot, Bert.'

'That's all right. And don't get into any more trouble.'

'I'm going straight back to my ship and stopping in my cabin until we sail for Rotterdam in the morning.'

He got out of the car and started walking. But he was still shaken and the desire for a drink possessed him. He went into a bar and after the first two whiskies felt better.

It was nearly midnight when he got back to his ship more than three parts drunk. But in some vaguely troubled way he was unable to banish the memory of the framed photograph. He was still seeing it when he fell into an alcoholic sleep.

10

Braxted announced: 'The preliminary report's in from the toxicologist.'

They were all in the shared office, Fallon drawing on an empty pipe, Brooker lighting a cheroot, Bawtry just craving to smoke. 'What's the strength of it, sir?' This from Brooker.

The Detective Chief Superintendent leaned forward, tapping the foolscap sheet with an index finger. 'This man died from a massive overdose of barbiturates taken either before or immediately after drinking, a fairish amount of drink — whisky.'

'That definitely lets Culley off the hook so far as murder is concerned.'

'Well, he was off it, anyway. We already knew the stab wound was a minor one.'

'On the face of things it doesn't even look like murder now. Are you saying it's a natural causes?'

'Accidental death would seem to be more like it.'

Fallon put his empty pipe away. 'It's common enough, fellas taking sleeping tablets after going on the booze, not knowing it could be fatal. But why the massive dose?'

'That's what's troubling me, Ted.'

'Happen it was suicide, then?'

Bawtry, who had not yet spoken, said slowly: 'It's feasible that a man fuddled with drink could take an overdose of sleeping pills, accidentally or on purpose. But he'd take them when he got inside.'

'You'd think so,' answered Braxted.

'Were the barbiturates themselves enough to kill him?' asked Brooker, stabbing the air with his small cigar.

'They're not absolutely positive about that, though it was a hefty overdose. But in conjunction with the heavy intake of spirits death was inevitable.'

'H'm.' Brooker sat with his hands dangling between his knees. 'This fella Leng could've been drunk enough to start swallowing pills on the way to his bedsitter, I mean when he was almost on the doorstep.'

'It's possible.'

'Would a man carry the things around with him, though?' queried Fallon.

Bawtry gave up trying not to smoke and lit a cigarette, the first of the day. Pity it couldn't be the last, he thought. '*If* Leng had barbiturates on him. But we found no bottle or packet. Which suggests he took them somewhere else.'

'That's what troubles me, Sam.' Braxted only used Bawtry's given name when he was warming to a line of discussion. 'Go on.'

'I'm considering the possibility that we still have a murder case on our hands, sir — that some person or persons unknown administered both the barbiturates and the whisky and then dumped Leng close to his room, probably still just about able to get upstairs.' Bawtry went on slowly: 'The one thing the killer couldn't possibly foresee was that Culley was going to stab Leng before he could get into his room. But for that it would've worked.'

'A simple plan,' mused Fallon. 'They're

always best. A fella found dead in his room from drink and an overdose of sleeping tablets. Inquest a formality, verdict a foregone conclusion.'

Brooker made a dry sound, midway to a chuckle. 'Happen we should thank young Culley, then, never mind book him.'

'He committed a serious offence, actual bodily harm, unlawful wounding. He'll have to go before the Stipe,' said Fallon.

'Of course, though it sounds a bit daft since Leng was already dying on his feet, or just about on his feet.'

Braxted pushed his shoulders against the padded back of his chair. 'We'll need to proceed carefully with this whole business. We've no real clue, never mind evidence. All we know is that Leng died from the combined effects of barbiturates and drink.'

'And that's how it would have stood if he hadn't been stabbed,' said Bawtry. 'More specifically — that's how the killer, if we're right about this, intended it to stand.'

'So all we have to do is find a

completely unknown murderer,' said Brooker sourly. 'Oh, sure, your Chinese pal says Leng mentioned a fella named Langley, but we've double-checked on every Langley on Merseyside and they're all as clean as whistles, never been within a thousand ruddy miles of Hong Kong, none of them. That makes the killer unknown.'

'Well, we've had *that* problem before,' remarked Fallon.

'Yes, we have, but this case beats the lot. We don't know where Leng went or where it happened. We're not even at square one.'

Braxted drummed fingers on his desk. When he spoke his voice had a tinge of irascibility. 'You don't have to state the difficulties, Brooker, they're self-evident.'

'I'm sorry, sir.'

The small vexation went away. 'You're stepping out of character, then.'

Brooker's mouth twitched faintly, but he said nothing.

The Chief Superintendent resumed: 'An all-out effort to trace the dead man's background. That's the first prerequisite.

Also, we'll get on to Interpol. They might know something.'

'Assuming he had a record with them.'

'If he hadn't we'll try the authorities in Hong Kong. In fact, we'll contact them in any case, find out what Leng did for a living, his known habits and associates, that sort of thing. It's at least possible that we might uncover something.'

'I'll have it put in hand,' said Fallon.

'Right. Meanwhile, we'll have fifty detectives detailed for inquiries throughout the city and Bootle, too. Brooker and Bawtry in charge.'

'Leng didn't disclose anything to Li Chou, apart from the fact that he was seeking this man he had known in Hong Kong, sir,' Bawtry observed.

'He might have spoken to other people. Suppose you try to find out.'

The conference broke up. In the big C.I.D. room Brooker set fire to another cheroot and said: 'It's easy Braxted telling us to launch massive inquiries, but where?' Answering himself, he said: 'All right, we'll have a picture taken of Leng and hawk copies round every pub and club on Merseyside. Somebody must've *seen* him, at least.'

'It'll do for a start. We can take the city centre between us and have prints sent to every bridewell with instructions for plainclothes men to work their own areas.'

'If Leng was a drinking man he must've been seen, but that doesn't necessarily mean he talked or was seen in public with this Langley fella. I'm not bloody optimistic, Sam.'

'It's all we've got to go on,' said Bawtry philosophically.

They got the prints inside half an hour. At opening time they started the pub crawl. Bawtry was working the area which crossed from Ranelagh Street through Clayton Square to Whitechapel, then up Lord Street towards the Pierhead. Nobody recalled having seen anybody who even looked like Tom Leng. By three-thirty in the afternoon they were back at Headquarters reporting the failure of a mission, with similar reports coming in from the bridewells.

'Happen we'll do better at night,' said

Bawtry. 'Not every fella starts drinking at lunchtime.'

'Not even me,' replied Brooker with a grin.

Bawtry went home to Carol. It was early, but he had telephoned her, timing the call so that she would be back from the hospital where she did part-time nursing. They still lived in the rather spacious flat which was his home in the days of his solitary batchelor existence. When they married he had suggested buying a home out in one of the suburbs, but Carol had fallen in love with the flat on the night she fell in love with Sam and he hadn't pressed the suggestion. It suited him in several ways, not least because it way only minutes from Headquarters and he liked the idea of being only minutes away from the beautiful girl who had become Mrs. Sam Bawtry.

'Why, Sam, it *is* nice to have you home early for once.' She gave him her arms and her mouth. He held her tightly, aware of what the physical contact was doing to him.

'I love you, I love you,' he said.

'It's very mutual, Sam.' She made her slightly throaty laugh. 'You aren't . . . not at this hour, surely?'

'Any time I catch sight of you.'

'And him an old married man,' she mocked.

'Just old.'

She put a hand up to his lips. 'Stop it, you're *not* old. How many more times have I got to tell you not to say that, not even to think it?'

'I'm fourteen years older than you.'

'What on earth does that matter?'

'It beats me.'

'What does?'

'I mean I can never work out what you see in me.'

'I love this touching humility. No, I don't,' she went on with feminine inconsistency. 'You simply have no idea what a terribly attractive man you are, Samuel Dennistoun Bawtry. What do you want to eat?'

'You, I think.'

'You only *think*?' She laughed again, dodging away from him. 'Fillet steak with chips and tomatoes, apple-pie and custard, coffee in the lounge in the best bone china cups, frightfully posh. Have you got that much time?'

Sam grinned. 'You ought to be a female cop instead of a nurse.'

'Just putting two and two together. Simple deduction from first causes or whatever it is you call it.'

'Meaning any time I come home early it's because I'm off out again.'

'Partly that, but also the look in your eye. And I don't mean *that* look, either.'

'Why, have I still got it?' asked Bawtry innocently.

'You can start setting the table if you want something to do,' said Carol austerely.

'I can rise above food.'

'I like that word rise.'

'Tut-tut!'

'But your amorous instincts won't stop you tucking into steak and chips.'

'Alas, no.'

'Now tell me why you're home early and going out again, probably not coming back until late.'

'Jacks don't talk about their work to the missus.'

'You do. Not often, but you do.'

'Yes, that shows I'm right under your thumb.'

'Ha, ha! Anyway, I'd hate to think you were. Not that there's any danger. *Are* you going to tell me?'

He told her, producing the photographic print. She looked at it for a moment, then said: 'I suppose he was dead when it was taken?' She made a small shiver.

'I'm sorry if it's upset you, love.'

'Not really, I've seen people dead before, often. It's just that the picture looks . . . sort of staring. Do you think you'll find someone who recognises it?'

'We'll try.'

She looked at it again and said: 'Have you got one to spare?'

'Why?'

'Three of the young housemen went out on a spree last night. They turned up this morning with the father and mother of a hangover. They might've noticed this poor man in one of the pubs they were in, which seems to have been most of them. I could show them the picture, just on the off-chance.'

'All right.'

They sat down to the meal. At six-thirty he kissed her and went out — 'I'll try not to be too late.'

'Come home sober if you expect to get any supper,' she called after him.

'What kind of supper?'

'Wait and see,' said Carol.

11

He retraced the route he had taken at lunchtime. Still nobody remembered seeing Leng. Bawtry wasn't put off. He'd have to try again and yet again, catching new batches of drinkers, including the lot who came in for the last hour, sinking pints with quiet desperation.

It was a quarter to nine when he thought of Big Dave McTaggart and the pub he invariably patronised about that time, a grim brass-railed Victorian boozer known as The Loops on a corner triangle between Strand Street and Nova Scotia, within sight of the Canning Dock.

The place was filling up when he got there. Cigarette smoke drifted in a dense pall above the heads of fifty men and a dozen women, most of them ravaged harridans, and even the younger ones carrying the unmistakable imprint of the oldest profession at its rock-bottom level.

Bawtry stood for a moment on the

threshold, aware that a score of eyes had seen him, some not caring, some with the furtive apprehension of men suddenly wishing they had gone to a different pub.

A huge back showed among a group at a corner table, down near the far end of the long bar. Bawtry thrust his way forward and said: 'Hello, Dave.'

The tearaway's enormous hand tightened on a new pint of black-and-tan. He came round slowly in his seat, looking up. 'Oh, it's you, Mr. B.' He said it without unbridled enthusiasm.

'Aren't you going to invite me to join the party, Dave?'

'Din't know you needed an invitation,' said McTaggart. 'Take a seat if you want, there's a space next to Ellie. You know my mates.'

'Very well indeed.' Bawtry sat next to the small wizened man whose full name, which was Jonathan Fortescue Ellsworth, had long since been foreshortened to Ellie except on those occasions when a charge was being read out to him, and the occasions had been many. The two others, Ginger Ducie and Jamie McCracken, eyed him with a nice blend of hostility and uneasiness as if they feared being discovered in the commission of some tort or malfeasance.

There was a prickly silence. Bawtry let it stay. Do no harm, make them jumpy. Big Dave ended it, his voice blaring like a foghorn on a Mersey ferryboat.

'Well, what's it all about, then?'

'What's what all about, Dave?'

'Don't give us that, Mr. B., you're not here to ask after our bleedin' health, you know that.'

'I might be.'

'Yeh, an' pigs might fly. You want summat from us, don't you?'

Bawtry lit a cigarette and blew the lighter flame out with calculated slowness. 'You might be able to give me a bit of information,' he said at last.

McTaggart's face, which had the general aspect of battle-scarred granite, twisted in a sneer. 'You don't want us to grass for you, do you?'

'If I did I'd know better than to ask,' replied Bawtry amiably. 'I know you lot and the peculiar code which governs your dubious ramifications.'

Ellie's voice, which resembled nothing so much as a petrified squeak, said: 'What's that mean when it's at home, then?'

'Yeh, talk English, can't you,' snarled Ducie.

'Not as we care,' said McCracken bitterly.

'I mean you fellas live in a nasty little world of petty crime where all differences are settled by the cosh and the bicycle chain with the boot put in at the finish.'

'We got our own law and order, you know that,' said McTaggart doggedly.

'Laughingly described as law and order,' said Bawtry. 'Law of jungle would be more like it.'

'What's all this got to do with whatever you're here for?' asked McTaggart savagely.

'Not a thing, Dave. I was just thinking aloud about the daft little private hell you fellas have made for yourselves. Always skint except when you've done a job. Tapping for loans, bluey thefts, a bit of housebreaking or robbery with violence, and the permanent fear of some cop feeling your collars and another stretch in Walton from the assize judge. Not much of a life, I'd have thought.'

'Better'n working for a snotty boss,' said McTaggart.

'You'd do better working on the docks, the way things are now, except that you might have trouble getting admitted to a respectable trade union.'

'I'll tell you summat,' said Big Dave. 'I've never worked in me life and I'm not starting, see? As to the Jacks feeling our collars that's just the risk we take.' He quaffed black-and-tan, passed the back of a coarsened hand across his mouth and said: 'Well, all right then, out with it.'

Bawtry grinned. The preliminary kidology, the talking the madam, had been satisfactorily disposed of according to protocol. The decks were cleared.

'Right. I want to know if any of you have seen this fella.' As he spoke Bawtry took one of the photographs from his inside jacket pocket and laid it flat on the beer-stained table.

Four heads craned over it. Three of them were shaken, without words. Not Ellie's.

Bawtry said: 'You've seen him, then?'

'I never said so . . . '

'You didn't have to. Where?'

'In a boozer, yesterday lunchtime.'

'What boozer?'

'Tolly Mellish's.'

It was a small pub about half-way between Old Hall Street and the Princes Dock. 'Tell me more, Ellie.'

The small man shrugged. 'I seen him, that's all. Or a fella like him.'

'You didn't know him?'

'No. I told you, I just happened to see him, that's all. He was having a drink and . . . ' Ellie stopped.

'And what?'

'Nowt.'

'You were going to say something.'

'A fella what looked like this picture was in t'pub, that's all I know.'

'Having a drink?'

'Yeh.'

'By himself?'

Ellie picked up his glass, just to have

something to do. Bawtry pressed the point: 'By himself or with somebody? And you'd better not lie about it.'

'I got nothing more to tell you, Mr. B.'

'You have if you don't want booking for obstructing a police officer in the execution of his duty.'

'You can't make that stick, I've done nowt.'

Big Dave said unexpectedly: 'Tell him, Ellie.'

The wizened man arched his skinny shoulders. 'If you say so, Dave. All right, this fella come in by himself, but after a bit he got talking.'

'Who with?'

'Terry Byass it was.'

'Do you mean they already knew each other?'

'I don't think they did, they just happened to get chatting over a drink, they was standing together in t'bar.'

'Why couldn't you have said so straight away?' Bawtry asked, though he knew why well enough: Byass was a villain like themselves and to talk about him might sound like grassing. It was funny, though, how Terry Byass's name kept cropping-up.

It was Big Dave who answered. 'You know us, Mr. B., we don't like talking to the Jacks about anyone we know.'

'You got Ellie to tell me, just the same.'

McTaggart shrugged. Bawtry thought: he's being a bit co-operative because he doesn't want any trouble just now. That means they're up to something or thinking of getting up to something. Aloud, he said: 'Did you overhear what they were saying, Ellie, or any part of it?'

'I wasn't near enough, Mr. B.'

Big Dave said curiously: 'Why d'you want to know about this fella in t'picture?'

Bawtry picked up the print and said: 'This man's name is Tom Leng. He was found dead in an entry off Pitt Street. Somebody had put a knife in him.'

McTaggart's jaw hardened, jutting out. 'What're you . . . '

'Don't get excited, Dave, you're not involved. We've already booked somebody for the stabbing.'

'Murder, is it?'

'Unlawful wounding, more like it. A minor injury.'

'I thought you said this fella was dead?'

'He is, but he was dying when the knife was put in him. Overdose of sleeping pills and whisky, that's what killed him.'

McTaggart's voice boomed, calling for another round. 'You want one, Mr. B.?'

'Not just now.'

'Suit your bloody self. What's it all about then, if it's just a natural causes?'

'We want to find anyone who knew this poor fella or had any conversation with him. You've told me, or Ellie has. I'm much obliged.'

Big Dave eyed him narrowly. 'There's more to it than you've let on, if you ask me,' he said.

'Ah, but I haven't, Dave.' Bawtry rose, looking down at them. 'If you lot are up to something, just call it off, eh?'

'We ain't done nothing,' muttered Ginger Ducie.

'That's fine. You all keep it that way and you don't have to eat that prison scoff again. Or not just yet. A very good day to you all,' added Bawtry, raising his hat.

He sauntered out of the bar, almost physically aware that four pairs of eyes were boring into his back, not affection-ately.

12

The gaunt house was still deserted. Happen Terry Byass was out with a new Judy or getting half-cut or breaking into a shop. Or even with his old fella, not that there was much love lost between father and son. Might be worth a visit, though.

Bawtry drove there, taking a few short cuts he knew, finally sliding alongside the kerb outside a grimy terrace in Santon Street, just south of Everton Valley. It was 9.57 p.m. and chinks of light showed behind heavy curtains. Bawtry banged a pitted knocker, the door opened about four inches and he was seeing Toby Byass for the first time in getting on for a couple of years. He hadn't changed, apart from putting a bit more fat on and he had enough to start with.

'Well, well!' said Toby Byass.

'I hope you are, Toby,' said Bawtry genially. 'Mind if I step inside?'

'What — me with the Jacks in t'house?'

Byass chuckled wheezily. 'The disgrace of it!'

'I didn't know you cared what the neighbours think.'

'There's an old goat lives across the way who's already taking it all in, Mr. B. Peeping from t'bedroom window, must've heard you drive up. It'll give her summat to gossip about for the next week. Come on in, then.'

Bawtry stepped straight into the parlour. The television was on with a sagging horsehair sofa facing the 23 inch screen and several bottles of light ale on a table, one of them newly-opened. Toby Byass waddled across and switched off *News at Ten* just as it got under way.

'Care to join me in a drink?'

'No thanks. You have one, though.'

'I was going to.' Byass poured into a tall clouded glass and added. 'I'm still working regular.'

'I'm glad, Toby.'

'I just want that understood, like.' Byass tipped the glass to his mouth, breathed out noisily and sat down, spreading both hands on thighs like tree trunks. 'If a bank job's come up you're wasting time seeing me.'

'So far as I know, all the banks in town are still *virgo intacta*.'

'Well, if one does get done just think on that it'll not be any of my doing, Mr. B.'

'Still retired, eh?'

'That's right.'

'Living quietly on your ill-gotten gains.'

'You don't expect me to answer that, now, do you?'

'Not even with a knowing look,' answered Bawtry cheerfully.

'I'm living on me rigger's pay and I draw the interest every half-year on a bit o' brass I've got put by in t'building society, all honest and above board, as you might say.'

'Except perhaps where it came from in the first place, but I'm not here about that.'

'You couldn't prove owt, not now,' said Toby Byass comfortably. 'Well, if it's not that, what is it?'

'I really came to see that lad of yours . . . ' Even as he spoke Bawtry saw the tight expression on the other's moon-like face.

Byass took a pinched-out cigarette from his shirt pocket, set fire to it and said harshly: 'What's he been up to, then?'

'Nothing unlawful, at least nothing we know about. I just want some information, that's all.'

'Well, he's not here.'

'So I gather, but he's not at his own place, either.'

'What place?'

'He's staying with that aunt of his out near Shiel Park. I thought you'd know.'

'I don't know what you're on about and that's a fact.'

'You mean he hasn't got an aunt?'

'There's me sister, but she lives at Widnes. Went there after my missus died and that's nigh on ten year since.'

Bawtry felt the small prickly sensation he invariably got when something was wrong and there was something wrong about this. He repeated the substance of what the old woman told him when he was out at Burnside Grove.

The ex-jelly man pitched his cigarette butt into the old-fashioned grate. 'We had a set-to, fortnight ago it was, and Terry took himself off. He must be lodging at this place.'

It was possible. Happen the woman who lived there had let off a room while she was away and put it about that she was letting it to a relative. The small sensation Bawtry had felt ebbed. He said: 'What were you and Terry brawling about?'

'Various things. We don't get on, if you must know.' Toby Byass hesitated, then said: 'I don't want him to end up spending half his life in stir.'

'Well, *you* haven't, Toby.'

The fat face split in a slow grin. 'You didn't always catch me, Mr. B., otherwise I would've done. But Terry isn't even half smart enough. He only thinks he is, the bloody little twit.'

'So you've been trying to reform him, have you?'

'Trying to keep him out of trouble, more like. But he'll not listen, he thinks he knows it all.'

'That's not uncommon among the young.'

'I dare say, but this is different. I mean he's liable to finish up doing a long stretch.' Toby shrugged. 'We had a blazing row about it and he slung his hook. I thought he was staying with Tommy Flynn, one of his mates.'

Bawtry stood up. 'I thought perhaps he might be here, seeing you. I'll just have to keep calling at this place he's got, that's all.'

'What d'you want him for, or aren't you telling?'

'No reason why not, Toby.' He explained briefly. 'It was probably only a casual exchange of words over a drink, but it's just possible this man Leng may have told him something.'

'Like the address of the fella he was looking for?'

'I'm not saying he did, but it's possible. If you see him tell him he's wanted at Headquarters and that he'd better come if he knows what's good for him.'

'I'll see he gets there if I have to frog-march him meself, Mr. B.'

Outside, Bawtry debated whether to go back to the house near Sheil Park but decided it would keep till morning. He drove home and Carol said: 'The phone just rang for you. Someone you know — Mr. Berkeley.'

'Charles Berkeley, the bank manager?'

'Yes, he said would you call him back as soon as you got in.'

'I'll do it now.' Bawtry dialled the number of the roomy flat Berkeley occupied above the Maritime and Asiatic Bank because it suited him not to have to drive in from some distant suburb.

His remembered voice came down the line. 'I'm sorry to trouble you, especially at this hour, but I'm a little worried. Could you drop round just for a few minutes?'

'I've only just got in, sir. You couldn't tell me what it is over the phone, could you?'

'Well, yes, but I'd prefer to tell you in person.' There was a small hesitation, then: 'It *is* rather important, Bawtry.'

'I'll come round, then.' He put the receiver down and said apologetically to

Carol: 'Berkeley seems to be bothered about something — wants me to call on him now.'

'Then you'd better go, Sam.'

'I'd sooner stay with you.'

'It's mutual, darling, but if he's worried . . . ' She wrinkled her slightly up-tilted nose. 'You did him a good turn on that case a year or two ago, didn't you?'

Bawtry nodded. Watching him, Carol thought: he's already half-way there in his mind. Who'd marry a Jack? I would, but only if it was this one.

Ten minutes later Bawtry was going into the wide lounge with its radio-gramophone and the bookcase lined with bound sets of Shakespeare and Dickens and a stack of crime fiction from the Sapper and Edgar Wallace periods.

Berkeley, a tall slightly stooping man in his late fifties with keen blue eyes behind gold-rimmed spectacles, said: 'Would you care for a Scotch?'

'If you're having one, sir.'

'Good. It's supposed to be easier to talk with a glass in one's hand and this isn't particularly easy for me.'

Bawtry said nothing. The bank manager poured the drinks and went on slowly: 'It's bank business and I'm probably doing something irregular in telling you. It will have to be in complete confidence. Is that possible?'

'If what you are going to say leads to subsequent criminal proceedings it could be difficult.'

Berkeley walked agitatedly across the hearthrug. 'I'll put it another way. If what I am about to confide leads to a prosecution could the information be described as from an undisclosed source?'

'Happen it could, sir. Depends on the circumstances.'

'You sometimes get what you call a tip-off without disclosing the source, don't you?'

'That's true.' Bawtry smiled faintly. 'In consequence of information received is the phrase. Anyway, I'll bend the rules as far as they'll go. Will that do?'

'I think so, yes.' Berkeley sat down and said: 'It concerns a client of the bank. A widow. She has £1,670 on deposit and has or had £1,200 on current account.'

'You used the past tense about the latter, sir.'

'Yes, in the past three weeks she has reduced her credit on current account to just under the two hundred pounds.'

'You'd better tell me the specific reason why this is worrying you, Mr. Berkeley.'

'The client has made out five cheques, each for quite a substantial sum, none of them to a firm or shop or anything like that. Also, she hasn't been down to the bank during this time, which is unusual because she normally calls in every Friday to pay in money from some rents she has, investment properties left by her husband. That's what bothers me. I should explain that the cheques were all made payable to the same person, who has an account at another bank.'

'And you think there's something odd about it?'

'I don't know exactly what to think. But, well, I'm rather perturbed.'

'I think,' said Bawtry quietly, 'that you'll have to tell me the name. Who were the cheques made payable to?'

'Somebody named Byass . . . '

Bawtry sat bolt upright. 'Give me the full name!'

'There was only an initial on the cheques — T. Byass.'

Bawtry put his drink down unfinished and rose fast. 'Is the client a Mrs. Millicent Jenkins, with an address in Burnside Grove?'

Berkeley twitched the gold-rimmed glasses off his nose, staring. 'You *know* her?'

'No, I've never met her, but I have reason to believe that a young criminal named Terence Byass is living in her house. I had occasion to call there and a neighbour said Mrs. Jenkins was away in Chester on an extended visit.'

'But . . . but that's impossible, the latest cheque was signed only today.' Berkeley's eyes widened. 'You . . . you mean . . . '

'I don't know, sir, but I'm going to find out — now!'

13

Bawtry walked back to Headquarters, arriving as one of the car crews came in, Collins and Armiston

'I want you lads to come with me to a house in Burnside Grove, near Sheil Park,' Bawtry said.

'We're just going off duty,' Bert Collins murmured.

'Well, you're back on it again. Any objections?'

'A few, including the fact that I'm about to start a bit of leave, but I'm not pressing it,' Collins said.

Bawtry tipped his hat off his forehead. 'Sorry, lads — but it may be important.'

'For you, anything, Mr. B. Who minds about going home?'

Bert Collins drove with Armiston in the front passenger seat and Bawtry in the back. It was nearing midnight and the traffic chaos of the day had gone.

'We're doing forty-eight in a restricted

area,' Collins observed.

'I didn't hear that,' said Bawtry. 'You must have been speaking into my deaf ear.'

'Didn't know you had one, Mr. B.'

'Nor did I.'

Collins chuckled and sent the car streaking up the West Derby Road. A police panda, about to nose out of a side street, halted, the driver watching them go past. When they got there the house still wore its abandoned look. A thin breeze came across the open dirt space, riffling discarded bits of paper.

Bawtry said tersely: 'Run the car round the back.'

'Right.' Collins let the car drift in, engine and lights off.

Bawtry said: 'We're going in.'

'Don't we need a warrant?'

'Not in these circumstances. Entering a house on suspicion that the occupant may have been taken ill and needs help. We'll try the back entrance.'

There was no garden, only a small irregularly-paved yard behind a high wall with a door in it. The door was locked and felt as if it was bolted.

'One of you give me a bunk up,' said Bawtry.

Collins bent a broad back, levering Bawtry high enough to get a purchase on the top of the wall. In another minute he had dropped down and was letting them into the yard.

The back door of the house was locked, but this time not bolted. Bawtry took the slim celluloid window from the driving licence slot of his wallet and slid the wards of the lock back.

They were in the kitchen. Armiston swivelled a hand torch round, found the wall switch and got lights on. A table set in the middle of the small room was littered with the remains of more than one meal and the single-drainer sink was stacked with unwashed dishes.

Bawtry, who was fastidious about hygiene, wrinkled his nose in distaste. There was no sound anywhere in the house except the audible ticking of a cheap alarm clock on the cluttered mantelpiece. But that meant that the clock had been wound up, recently.

170

He opened the door on to a short hall leading to the front of the house and switched more lights on. There were two other rooms, a dining-room and a front parlour with a dusty aspidistra in a green window tub.

'Place seems deserted,' Armiston said.

'We'll try upstairs — and switch all the lights off first.'

'Right.' Armiston sent the slim beam of his torch spearing ahead as they climbed ten stairs going straight up and four more round a left-hand bend which brought them on to a red-carpeted landing. As they reached it Bawtry stiffened.

'Somebody's in the front room,' whispered Collins. 'I heard a sound.'

Bawtry's big hand closed down on the trigger handle of the door. There was a small click, then a choked cry like terror made audible. He slammed the door inwards, standing aside as Armiston's torch probed the darkness.

A woman was lying on the bed. Words came from her: 'Please . . . please don't hurt me again.'

Bawtry reached for the wall switch and

thumbed it down. The sudden light showed them a woman in her late fifties, a thin woman with short grey hair and a face without colour except where livid welts showed down one side. Her hands were behind her back, her ankles corded.

'It's all right, ma'am — we're police.'

'Oh, thank God . . . ' The words ended in the flood-release of sobbing.

Bawtry slashed the bonds and propped her gently against the pillows. 'You're safe, love. Mrs. Jenkins isn't it?'

She nodded, then clutched at him, not crying now but trembling violently, beyond control. Then that stopped, too.

'Who marked you?' asked Bawtry.

'A young man, I don't know him, I never saw him until he called at the house . . . don't let him get at me again.'

'He'll not get at anything except sewing mailbags,' said Collins.

Bawtry said: 'He committed violence to force you into signing cheques payable to him. That's right, isn't it?'

'Yes, how do you know?' She winced. 'There's other marks, on my back, where he beat me.'

Armiston said savagely: 'I'll give him summat to remember when he comes back, missus.'

'Understandable reaction — but we do this according to the book,' replied Bawtry. 'When's he coming, then?'

'I don't know, he comes back all times, mostly late at night or in t'small hours.'

'It's nearly that now. Why didn't you shout for help when he went out these last few nights?'

'There's no houses near, sir. Besides, he threatened what he'd do to me . . . ' She moistened her lips. 'I was too terrified to do it, anyway.'

Bawtry looked at his watch. Fifteen minutes past midnight. He crossed to the window and parted the curtains enough to look out. A car engine sounded, out of sight, changing down on an exhaust note like a sports model.

'Put the light out, Bert!'

The room went dark, like the rest of the house. Bawtry said: 'We have to prove that this man is holding you prisoner and has committed violence against you. To do that we have to catch him — here, with you. Do you understand, Mrs. Jenkins?'

'Yes.' The word was less than a whisper.

'We'll wait in the other bedroom until he comes in here. Will you co-operate?'

'I'll try, sir.'

'He won't hurt you again, love, that's a promise. But I'll have to tie you up again.'

A car stopped outside the house. Footsteps came, then the small sound of a key turning in the front door lock.

'It's him, the stinking bastard.' This from Collins.

They went into the other bedroom, crossing the carpeted landing without sound, and stood behind the door, not quite closed.

Down below a voice called: 'It's me, auntie, your long-lost nephew what never was come back for a little chat — a little chat and a big cheque.'

Terry Byass turned the bend in the stairs and walked down the landing into the front room. The lights came on again.

'You've still got a bit left, auntie, but you'll not have it after tonight. One more cheque and you'll never see your ever-loving nephew again.' His speech was slurred with booze.

'You're not my nephew,' said Millie Jenkins.

'Oh — so you're arguing now, are you? We'll soon put a stop to that.'

'I'm giving you no more money . . . '

'Belt up, auntie.' He laughed. 'Belt is dead right — that's what you're going to get, like I gave it you before. A right belting until you sign away the rest of the lolly.'

He unbuckled the studded leather belt round his waist, swinging it.

Bawtry slid out of the room and stood in the doorway. 'Hello, Terry,' he said.

Terry Byass stood there, half-crouching, frozen in his last arrested attitude. Then he screamed, a single rising dissonance as he swung completely round, flailing the studded belt.

Bawtry lunged sideways, then tore in, diving below the lashing belt. The juddering impact sent the other flat against the wall, spreadeagled.

'You lousy pig, I'll kill you!'

As he yelled Terry Byass went for a

flick-knife. Bawtry's hand closed like a steel trap on his wrist, forcing it down, then making a full arm-lock, almost to snapping point. Terry Byass screamed again.

'Put the handcuffs on him, Bert.'

There was a metallic click. Terry Byass swayed madly, staring at his manacled wrists. 'I'll bloody murder you, Bawtry!'

'So you keep saying, but you'll have to wait a while.'

'Years, we hope,' said Armiston.

Millie Jenkins was standing unsteadily by the side of the bed, a freed hand on the headboard. She looked at Terry Byass for a long moment.

'How could you do this to me? I've done nothing to you, I never saw you in my life before you came to my door.'

Terry Byass spat on the floor.

'I'm sorry for you,' said Millie Jenkins simply.

★ ★ ★

They threw the book at him: demanding money with menaces, possessing an

176

offensive weapon, causing actual bodily harm, resisting arrest. Enough to put him down for a long stretch, unless the jury fell for a plea of schizophrenia or some other psychiatric malaise. But there wasn't likely to be one because Terry Byass wouldn't want his mates to think he was even half bent. He had to play the big fella, the free-spending good-time Charley who thumbed his nose at the Jacks even when they booked him.

Braxted, who had looked in at Headquarters on the way home from a civic function, said: 'Good work, Sam. You say Byass was seen talking to Leng. I take it you haven't had time to go into that yet?'

'I'm about to, sir.'

'I'll be in my office for half an hour or so. It might take you longer, though.'

'I doubt it,' said Bawtry. He went through to the interview room. Terry Byass was sitting on the other side of the small table, no longer playing the big fella. He had run out of defiance since they slapped the charges on him.

Bawtry decided to make it brief, even to the point of menace. 'I want some information from you and I want it quick, no messing.'

'You've booked me, what more d'you want?'

'A man named Tom Leng died after being stabbed in an entry off Pitt Street. You were seen talking to him in a pub near Central Station. Why?'

Terry Byass shook. 'You lousy Jack — what're you trying to do?'

'I just told you. I'm waiting for an answer.'

'I don't know no Tom Leng, I never heard of him, I tell you.'

'You spoke to him in this boozer. It can be proved.'

'You can eff off . . . '

'I'm investigating a murder, Terry — the murder of a man last seen in your company.'

'Gimme a cigarette,' said Terry Byass thickly. Bawtry pushed the packet across the table, followed it with a held lighter. Terry Byass poked the cigarette in the small flame. The cigarette shook in his mouth. He dragged on the smoke, coughingly. 'You're trying to bloody frame me.'

'A man has been murdered. You spoke to him. I want to know about that — here and now!'

Terry Byass shouted: 'I tell you I don't know no fella of that name.'

'A man in his thirties, face sort of very faintly coloured, not white. Blue suit, white shirt, very black hair — almost blue-black.' He paused as dawning recognition showed in the other's eyes. '*Did* you know him?'

'No. I did speak to a fella like that, though. It was just a bit of a chat at t'bar. He didn't tell me his name and I didn't ask. It was nowt.'

'What *did* he say?'

'You've got me slated for at least three years in Walton — why the hell should I help *you*?'

'No reason.'

Terry Byass looked at the tip of his cigarette, then up. 'You could go a bit easier on me in return for summat, couldn't you?'

'I could, but I'm not even considering it.'

'Get bloody lost then.'

Bawtry said: 'Do you want some tea?'

'No, I don't.'

'Better have a cuppa. Helps thought, tea. Better than booze. Doesn't cloud the mind. You need a clear mind just now, never more so, eh?'

'You — '

'Your addiction to basic Anglo-Saxon is getting monotonous.' Bawtry nodded to the uniformed constable, who went out and came back with two mugs of tea.

'You might as well sup some of this, it's better than you'll get at Walton, though not much,' said Bawtry.

'Funny!'

'You're not in a funny position, Terry. Up before the Stipe in the committal court, then in custody to the next Assizes.'

Terry Byass's eyes narrowed. 'Whose t'judge going to be?'

'Mr. Justice Egrison.'

'Jesus!'

'The judge is getting a reputation for

putting down violence. Stiff sentences. Add to your recent crime the fact that you withheld information needed in a murder case and his lordship is liable to give you the longest sentence on record.'

Terry Byass said huskily: 'I was only joking, I mean about not talking.'

'Aye, well, the joke's over now, in more ways than one.'

'I only had a few words with this fella, but I reckon you'll not believe me, not now.'

'Try me.'

'What d'you want me to say then?'

'I'm not asking you to make anything up, Terry. I simply want you to remember, as close as you can, what was actually said between you and Leng.'

'I'll have some tea,' Terry Byass said. He drank about half of what was in the mug and went on: 'It was nothing much, just chat about t'weather and beer. He said he'd been out in t'Far East and missed English wallop. That sort of chat. The only other thing he said was that he was expecting to be on Easy Street now that he was back from wherever it was.'

'Hong Kong.'

'He didn't say that, he just said t'Far East.'

'And he was expecting to be on Easy Street — those were his exact words?'

'Yeh.'

'He didn't go into detail about how he expected this to come about?'

'No, but he said he was meeting a fella about it next day.'

'Who and where?'

'How the hell should I know? He just said it was going to be all right for him and winked. I wasn't even listening, not proper. I thought he'd had a few and was trying to put it on a bit, like.'

Bawtry thought: a man named Leng comes back to Liverpool from Hong Kong, talks about going to be on Easy Street and seeing someone important the next day, somebody we don't know living we don't know where. And the following night he gets killed. Bloody marvellous. All we have to do is find this contact — just like that!

Bawtry stood up. Terry Byass said: 'I've told you all I can, I've done me best. I hope you'll do t'same for me.'

'You'll get your just deserts for what you did to Mrs. Jenkins, but you've not made it a sight worse for yourself by withholding information, such as it's turned out to be,' replied Bawtry and went out.

He was in the detectives' room when Information came on with a report that the night watchman at the Northern Commerce Bank in Altcar Street had been attacked but had managed to touch-off the alarm system and the intruder had fled.

Bawtry walked into the Information Room. Jenny Mycroft, who was on late radio duty, said: 'I thought you'd be home by now, Mr. Bawtry.'

'So did I, but events arranged themselves differently. Any more about this bank business?'

'No. G Division are investigating. Do you want to join in?'

'I don't think so, not if Don Toleman's in charge.'

'Superintendent D. R. Toleman has taken over in person, assisted by the following staff from the bridewell — Inspector Drury, recently transferred from 'C' Division, Sergeant Dockerty and four constables,' intoned Jenny Mycroft.

'Then they'll not need help from Headquarters,' grinned Bawtry. 'Anyway, the fella didn't get away with anything. How's the watchman, though?'

'Not hurt. The intruder, who was masked, tied him up, that's all, but he managed to struggle free and get to the alarm.'

Bawtry went home to Carol. It was after one o'clock in the morning and he was tired, but not too tired.

14

Matt Lancing was home, too. Alone, and not so much tired as scared. Della was visiting friends in Nottingham; that was why he had picked this time to get into the bank, not that he any longer needed to alibi himself for being out. Better if she was away, though. It had seemed a good idea — get into the bank by a ruse, find the safety deposit section and somehow get that incriminating file out. Only it wasn't really a good idea, he knew that when he got inside. Out of his line, a hundred miles out. He hadn't the expertise. So he had changed the plan — hadn't even tied the watchman up properly and the bloody alarm had gone and he had cut and run for it. Not before he had figured out for himself where the safety deposit section was, though, but much good that was going to do him now. The only saving fact was that the watchman couldn't identify him behind

185

the nylon stocking he wore as a mask, nobody could. That was the one smart thing he'd done, not even nicking one of Della's stockings in case she asked where it had gone. He had bought a pair in a shop near the St. John's shopping precinct. The girl assistant had asked him what size and he hadn't known and a woman next to him had asked how tall his wife was and suggested a size.

Though he cared little about drinking, he poured himself a stiff brandy and sat in the lounge struggling with his thoughts. Somehow, he didn't even begin to know how, he still had to get that file out of the bank. It was no use trying again himself, he had learned that much. He was all right with the old con business, all suave charm and invigorating reassurance, nobody to touch him. Never been put down by the law — apart from that affair in St. Louis never within sight of it. Despite the murders he had committed, away from the smooth angles of crime he was out of his depth. He'd never even have gone to the bank but for the desperate knowledge of what Della had done. As long as what she had written down stayed in the safety deposit he couldn't even risk absconding.

He finished his drink and paced restlessly up and down the room, smoking cigarettes in jerky inhalations and grinding them out unfinished. Thirty-seven minutes later he was no closer to a solution.

Words came from him, audibly, hanging in the air as if they had been spoken by someone else, a disembodied voice: 'I've *got* to get it, I can't wait much longer. I can't cover for more than a week or two now, if that. I daren't risk another near-disaster like tonight. It's a job for a professional . . . '

He stopped pacing the room. A professional . . . he almost rolled the words round his tongue. An expert who could get inside and do a quick, clean job. Well, perhaps not that quick because it'd take time, but a clean skilled job, no clues left. Who? Something stirred in his mind, the recollection of something he had heard on a business trip to London. He had gone into a pub off Poland Street and found himself standing next to an expatriate Liverpudlian with an unstoppable flow of racy stories about jacks and knaves on Mersey-side. Lewey Flude. He didn't know him from Adam, but they had a couple of drinks together and a lot of chat, most of it one-sided.

He'd mentioned that he lived in Liverpool and Flude had said humorously: 'If you ever want to bust a bank up there get hold of Toby Byass — the best jelly man of the lot.'

Matt remembered asking: 'How do *you* know?'

Flude laughed. 'Ask any of the C.I.D., they'll tell you. Not even the great Sam Bawtry has put the arm on Toby Byass in years.'

'You sound as if you might be in the police yourself,' said Matt, though that wasn't what he thought.

Lewey Flude had grinned knowingly and switched the talk to women, a subject which he seemed likely to expand indefinitely, but Matt had looked at his watch and said: 'Must be going, got a train to catch.'

That was more than a year ago and he hadn't even thought of the conversation since. But now it all came back. He got the telephone book off a shelf and leafed through the 'B' section. Nobody named *Byass, T.* listed. It didn't matter, there were other ways. First thing in the morning he'd get hold of a street directory.

He undressed and got into bed and slept.

★   ★   ★

Another fine, clear day warmed by unclouded sunshine. But the climate at the morning conference was less than sunny. Braxted was in one of his slightly irascible moods; they weren't frequent but when he had one coming on subordinates tended to play things close to the waistcoat.

He looked round the shared office, his gaze shifting in turn to Fallon, Brooker and Bawtry, each deliberately quiet, waiting. It was understood, as if by some private telephathic communication, that the Detective Chief Superintendent was to have the floor.

'For God's sake, Ted, *must* you smoke that damned stuff in here?' Braxted demanded testily.

Fallon, who had fed his special brand of shag tobacco into a blackened pipe and set fire to it, hit a few dancing sparks with the desk blotter and laid the offending briar down. His over-long face carefully preserved its customary aspect of mild sadness, except for a barely perceptible upward twitch at one corner of his mouth.

'You want to chuck that stuff in the Mersey and get on to these things,' remarked Brooker, sliding the first cheroot of the day from its transparent cylinder. 'On second thoughts perhaps not — might complete the destruction of all marine life.'

Braxted made a reluctant grin. 'If you chaps insist on smoking at conference I'll have to light a cigarette in self-defence.' Braxted was next-door to being a non-smoker and if he was going to light up it was a signal that the small irascibility was passing.

Silently, Bawtry passed a new packet of twenty Players across the desk. The Chief Super took one, looking at Bawtry, who shook his head. 'I'm trying not to smoke till mid-day, sir.'

'Well, *I'm* not doing it because I like it, Sam.' The use of Bawtry's given name banished the last traces of tension.

Brooker led straight in. 'Detailed lab report on Leng. Massive overdose of barbiturates taken either before or immediately after consumption of whisky equal to approximately five doubles. If he took the barbiturates after drinking or the other way round why should he be in the entry?'

'Might've come down for something,' said Fallon stolidly. He picked up his pipe, not lighting it. 'Unlikely, though.'

'We can't rule out the possibility, Ted.' Braxted drummed fingers on the desk. 'Just the same, we'll treat this at least as a suspected case of murder. The trouble is we're not getting anything like proof.'

Brooker studied the tip of his small cigar, looked up and said drily: 'How many people who've died from a combination of drink and drugs were, in fact, murdered?'

'That's hypothetical.'

'We're looking at theories, sir. The point remains and could be applied to these specific circumstances. Also, it could be the easiest way of getting rid of someone.'

'It was your theory in the first place, Sam,' observed Braxted. 'What's your view now?'

'Unchanged, sir.'

'Leng might knowingly have taken drink and drugs in large quantities with the intention of suicide. Conversely, he might have taken them without understanding the lethal effect. In either case he could have left his room to call help — a doctor.'

'Except that if he wanted to ring-up a doctor there was a telephone on the landing, a coin-box.'

'He could have been in a panic.'

'There's also the point that he was apparently expecting to be on Easy Street financially. If so why should he even think of taking his own life?'

Braxted ground his unfinished cigarette out, making a wry face. 'On balance, I go along with your theory.'

Bawtry fingered his plain gold cuff-links, a small mannerism of which he was quite unaware. 'If it was murder the administration of the barbiturates could have been done without the victim knowing anything about it.'

'Slipping the stuff in his booze, like a Mickey Finn,' said Brooker.

'Exactly like that, almost certainly in the final drink because by then Leng would be even more unlikely to notice anything. Another point: barbiturates come in soluble form. At least four groups — nembutal, sodium amytal, sodium phenobarbitone and seconal. Any one of these would do.'

'Too much over-prescribing of the damned muck these days,' growled Brooker.

'Sleeping pills, tranquilisers and anti-depressants have their proper medicinal uses, you know,' said Braxted.

'I dare say, but the fact remains that in

a single year there were seventeen million prescriptions for barbiturates alone and an average of eighty tablets for each prescription. Any one prescription would be enough to kill half a bloody regiment.'

'That's a slight exaggeration,' grinned Fallon.

'Yes, it is, but you know what I mean. According to the lab fellas a dose of 260 milligrammes taken after all that Scotch would guarantee a one-way ticket to the next world.'

'So all we have to do is check on seventeen million prescriptions all over the country?'

'I think the killer is living in Liverpool,' said Bawtry. 'That much seems reasonably certain from what Leng let slip to Terry Byass in the pub, saying he was seeing somebody and hinting about there being money in it.'

'Blackmail,' said Brooker cosily.

'Happen, though it could be something else. Like revenge. Whatever it was, we have a situation in which a man is presumed to have been murdered shortly after announcing that he was looking for somebody named Langley on Merseyside.'

'We could check on every barbiturate prescription made up in the last few months,' mused Brooker. 'It'll take time, though — time enough for the killer to put a thousand miles between us and him, if he hasn't already done it.'

'I doubt that. Leng was murdered because he was a threat to someone. Once Leng was removed the need for instant flight would cease.'

'I'll arrange for a check,' said Fallon. He eyed Bawtry for a second, adding: 'I have an idea that you don't expect much from it, Sam.'

'I'm doubtful. It's possible that the killer got supplies from another part of the country, or even outside this country altogether.'

Braxted's head turned sharply. 'Are you on to something you haven't told us?'

'I wish I was, sir. I'm merely considering the fact that Leng came here from Hong Kong. It's at least possible that the man he was seeking also came from there.'

'God Almighty!' exploded Brooker.

'I'm not saying it as a fact, but I think we ought to look into it as a distinct possibility.'

'How do we start finding *that* out?'

'If we knew the answer to that the rest would be comparatively easy. Still, we ought to try.'

'How?' persisted Brooker. It was his turn to show irritability, a trait which tended to emerge when a case started to get difficult.

'Happen something'll turn up,' said Bawtry.

'What do we do, then — sit around on our backsides like bloody Micawber?'

'Perhaps something a bit more active than that,' answered Bawtry equably.

'Perhaps isn't going to help, Sam. The plain truth is that we haven't a clue, much less anything that even begins to look like evidence.'

'We'll get it, we usually do.'

'Not in every case. We're not damned infallible and there's more than one unsolved case on the files, you know that.'

'We have a new one now, the abortive

raid on the bank,' reflected Fallon.

'So we have and there's something funny peculiar about *that*,' said Brooker. 'One thing's for sure — it wasn't our old friend Toby Byass back on the job.'

'Someone manages to get into a bank and ties up the watchman. The watchman struggles free, sounds the alarm and the intruder runs for it,' mused Braxted. 'What does that suggest, would you say?'

'A botch-up,' sneered Brooker. 'An amateur.'

'Not necessarily. After all, he did get into the place,' said Fallon. 'Probably, though. Fella had enough nous to get in but not much else, eh?'

'If he'd been a real pro he'd have made sure the watchman couldn't get free.' Brooker mashed the stub of his cheroot into a splayed brownish mass. 'We know he wore a nylon mask and must've worn gloves because he left no dabs. Doesn't change his amateur status, though. Everybody knows about stocking masks and gloves these days. Where do we start looking for this comedian?'

'We don't,' replied Braxted. 'Superintendent Toleman is in charge and all bridewells notified. Of course, if we run across anything or have any ideas we can join in.'

'Not our worry,' said Brooker. 'We've a bigger one.'

A small silence hung in the air. Bawtry ended it. 'I'd like to have a word with the bank watchman.'

'You're already working on the Leng case,' Braxted reminded him.

'Very well, sir.'

'Oh, I'm not objecting, Sam, if you think you might get something. You're the best at the interrogation. No reason why you shouldn't take enough time out to see this watchman. Combining the two, as it were, eh?'

The words were said without meaning, but for a small irrational moment Bawtry felt something stirring in his mind, something he hadn't considered. It was ridiculous, though. What possible point of contact was there between Leng's murder and a botched-up bank job? It was just a crazy thought coming unbidden. He dismissed the notion and went out.

The night watchman was still in bed, in a terrace house at the bottom of a *cul-de-sac* off Lodge Lane between Vandyke Street and Aspen Grove. Walter Bledstowe, a gaunt gangling man with a cast in his left eye and a permanent stoop as soon as he stood up and started walking about.

His wife, a broad-featured woman of splendid proportions, said: 'I'll get Wally down for you, he'll not be a minute. Would you like some tea? Kettle's on.'

'I'd love it, ma'am.'

She went into the kitchen and Bawtry sat on a horsehair sofa. The house was on the wrong side of the street to catch the morning sun, so that the room seemed almost half-dark. Even the green plants rising from an ornamental bowl on a small mahogany table strategically positioned in the window bay took on a faintly sinister aspect. Or am I letting my imagination play about a bit? Bawtry grinned privately at the thought.

Letting his imagination roam was something he did fairly often. Walking alone through the streets of the city he sometimes amused himself by looking at passers-by and trying to deduce their occupations and private tastes and how the elderly ones must have looked when they were young. Of course, you could be entirely wrong, but sometimes you were almost startlingly right. He remembered a chance encounter in a hotel with a big, well-dressed man he had never met in his life; something about him had started Bawtry pondering. Ridiculous it was — but in the end he was the man they had almost literally given up hope of arresting for a break-in more than two years before at a shipping magnate's house up on The Drive.

The recollection of it came back to him as his gaze wandered round the neat, dim room. Not that there was anything here, anything to fire a train of deductive speculation. Just a small plain room, scrupulously clean, the curtains newly washed, no dust. Then the door opened and Wally Bledstowe shambled in, not yet wholly awake.

'Sorry to disturb you, Mr. Bledstowe.'

'Oh, that's all right. Only I don't usually get up this early, with working nights.' The gangling man peered through bifocal glasses. 'I remember you when you were walking a beat,' he offered. 'Gone up in t'world since then, eh?'

'Not to the dizziest heights,' said Bawtry amiably.

'You've not done so bad, lad.' The gaunt face showed a fleeting smile. 'I used to see a lot of you fellas when they had slops walking a beat, more'n they have today I mean. That's how I remember you. I used to think there's a smart young chap, he'll make his mark all right. What can I do for you?'

'To be frank, I don't really know, Wally. I just wondered if there's anything you might've noticed about this man who tied you up.'

'I told the local police station all I know, Mr. Bawtry.' There was a small stiffening in his voice.

'I didn't imagine you were keeping anything back,' said Bawtry. 'I just wondered if you might've recalled anything since you made a statement — any

201

small thing which might have come to you later.'

'Oh, I see what you mean.' The gaunt man passed a curled index finger across his long upper lip. 'I can't think of owt. This fella had one of them stocking things over his face, you know that.'

'I wasn't expecting you to describe his facial appearance,' Bawtry said. 'Let's try another angle. What kind of suit was he wearing?'

'Just a suit, navy blue or dark grey. Light wasn't too good and, besides, he sort of took me from behind.'

'His build, then?'

'About five-ten or eleven, but I said that in t'statement.'

'Did he strike you as a powerful man?'

'Fairy strong, I'd say, from t'way he grabbed me. Like a vice it was.'

A tall strong man in a dark suit with a fierce grip. For God's sake, it could be anybody.

'Did he speak?'

'Once, yes.'

'You didn't put that in your statement, Wally.'

'Didn't I?' Wally Bledstowe looked surprised. 'I thought I did.'

'What did he say?'

'Just that I wouldn't get hurt if I kept quiet and didn't struggle.'

'His voice, what was it like?'

'Bit on t'deep side.'

'Did he have a Liverpool accent?'

'Like a real Scouser, you mean? No, it was more — well, sort of a posh voice. Like some of them fellas you hear on't telly.'

A tall strong man with an educated voice. It wasn't much, but it was something. Find a well-spoken man in a dark suit. How?

'You're quite sure he didn't say anything else, Wally?'

'Certain. He just said to keep quiet and went off.'

'To where the strong-room is, you mean?'

'I suppose so, I'm not sure. I was getting me hands free. As a matter of fact, I thought he was near where the safety deposits are kept. Happen he didn't know properly where to start looking. Your fellas think he was just an amateur, don't they?'

'He didn't speak again while he was doing this or . . . ' Bawtry stopped. 'Something's come back to you, Wally.'

'It's nowt, not really. I mean he never spoke again, but he sort of hummed as he went about t'place like a fella humming to himself without knowing he was doing it.'

'You mean he was humming a tune?'

'That's right.'

'Can you put a name to it?'

'Not a name, but I know the tune all right.'

'Hum it for me.'

Wally Bledstowe chuckled. 'I've a voice like a bloody corncrake.'

'Try.'

The gaunt man puckered his lips. 'It goes *Da-da-da, da-dah da-de, da-da da-dah* . . . '

'The waltz theme from *The Merry Widow*,' said Bawtry.

'Aye, that's it, I'd forgot. He kept humming it.'

'And that's all?'

'I can't think of owt else, except that I

managed to get to the alarm, but you know all that.'

Bawtry stood up, swinging his hat. 'You've done your best and you *have* told me something, Wally.'

'It's still not much, though, is it?' said Wally Bledstowe as his wife came in with the tea.

Bawtry took a cup and then drove back to Headquarters.

'A tall comedian with a bit of a lah-di-dah voice who hums the *Merry Widow* waltz,' said Brooker. 'Jesus — we'll need more than that.'

'Fellas have betrayed themselves on less,' said Bawtry.

15

Toby Byass was having a day off and skimming through the racing sections of the three morning papers he took when the knock came on the front door. He opened it half-expecting to see Sam Bawtry on the step, this time about Terry being held in the main bridewell. Not that he cared over-much about his son's plight, largely because he had an ingrained dislike of the violence he knew Terry not only accepted but boasted about. Even in his late profession Toby Byass had been a man of peace, willing to go quietly on a fair cop — though he had mostly been astute or lucky enough to dodge the necessity, finally retiring into private life on the carefully hoarded and even more carefully hidden loot accumulated in fifteen years of immunity which had taken him dangerously into half a dozen cities and safely out of them.

He had never got on with his son since

Terry was in his early teens, too tall for his age, ceaselessly insolent and with a streak of cruelty in his nature which had come — from where? That was something which had always puzzled Toby. It hadn't come from him nor from the lad's mam. There must've been something way back, bad blood in some ancestor. It didn't matter. Nothing about Terry mattered, not even the fact that he was surely going down for a long stretch, unless some trick-cyclist got him off — boy deprived of mother's influence, childhood mal-adjustment to society and all that balls. Toby Byass shared with the older kind of hook the orthodox belief that if you were copped you simply took your medicine, no hard feelings and no whining. *If* you were copped, that is. He'd been too smart by half for the Jacks and Terry hadn't, the nit.

All these thoughts sped through his mind as he opened the door to find himself looking at a tall, well-built man he had never seen before.

'Are you Mr. Byass?' The voice went with the man's appearance, a bit on the deep side, nicely modulated without being affected. Some welfare Charley, thought Toby sardonically as he nodded, but the man's next words put that idea to flight. 'My name is Smith. I'd like to discuss a small matter of business with you — that is, if you've no objection.'

'Business — what business?' asked Toby guardedly.

'Just a matter of business which could be worth quite a handsome fee to you, Mr. Byass.'

'You're not selling owt, are you?'

'Do I look like a door-to-door salesman?' asked Matt Lancing.

Toby eyed him upwards from the polished black slip-on shoes to the medium-weight blue suit and the dark silk tie flat on a sheer white shirt. He didn't answer.

'I promise that you won't regret talking to me, Mr. Byass — on the contrary.'

Toby made a gesture. 'All right, you can come inside.' He opened the door wider, then closed it and followed the stranger into the kitchen. 'What's it all about, then?'

Matt glanced round the room, less than impressed by its basic functionalism. He wondered whether he'd come to the right place. Suppose there was another Byass? No, that was out, there was only one listed in the street directory. He was at the right place; better make sure, though — without mincing words.

'I understand that you are by way of being an expert with safes, Mr. Byass.'

Toby's face went totally blank; whatever expression there had been on it died as swiftly as if it had been poleaxed — a schooled reflex more significant than if he had spoken at length and with eloquence.

'I see that you grasp my meaning,' Matt said evenly. 'Don't worry, I'm not from the police.'

Toby Byass found his voice in a fractured sentence: '*Who told you about me?*'

'A man who used to live in Liverpool, I ran into him by chance in London. Name's Flude.'

'Lewey Flude — that loud-mouth!'

'You know him?'

'I knew him when he was up here, not

well, but I knew him. All chat is Lewey Flude.'

'He chatted about you.'

'Yeh — what of it?''

'Let's not beat about the bush, Mr. Byass. He said that if ever I wanted a safe opening you were the best man in the country to do it, bar none. He said it half-jokingly, but it's true, isn't it?'

For the first time something close to a smile moved on the other's moonlike features, but he remained silent.

'You don't need to be cagey, not with me,' Matt said.

'I got nowt to tell you, mate.'

Matt took a roll of notes from his inside jacket pocket, counted out a hundred in fives and put them on the table. 'That's a retainer, you keep it whether you accept the commission or not.'

The roly-poly man stared down at the money, as if fighting an inner battle with it. The money won, the way it always does, thought Matt.

'What do you want me to do,' asked Toby.

'It's a bank job.'

Toby laughed, a fat wheeze of sound without humour. 'I'd better tell you right off — I've quit. I gave it up years ago.' He poked hungry fingers at the money, then abruptly withdrew them. 'You can keep your brass, I'm not risking a bank robbery, no matter what the final cut is. There's summat you don't know, summat that loud-mouth didn't tell you — I've never been put down in years and I'm not sticking my neck out after all this time.'

'You won't be, Mr. Byass. I don't want you to steal the bank's money, either alone or with me. What I have in mind is a very unusual commission.'

Toby Byass took a battered tin from the mantelpiece, opened it and started rolling a cigarette, very thin with tobacco strands flaking from one end. When he lit it sparks ascended. 'Go on, then.'

Matt Lancing said levelly: 'I want a top man to get into a bank, open up a safety deposit and remove a file of papers. The deposit is numbered DL5. I don't want any chance of a slip-up so I need an acknowledged expert. You fit.'

'I get inside, open the safety deposit

and take these papers for you and that's all?'

'That's all.'

'How much?'

'Five thousand pounds in money changes hands the moment you deliver the papers.'

Toby ranged round the small room dragging on his raddled cigarette. Watching him, Matt thought: he's going to stall but in the end he'll do it.

'I'm clean with the Jacks and I don't want putting down for a bank steal,' the fat man said.

'They never arrested you?'

'Once, fifteen year ago. They couldn't make the charge stick. Nothing since.'

'You must have been a hell of a smart operator,' said Matt admiringly. A bit of the old flannel never did any harm.

Toby produced a smile that was not quite a smirk. Then it went as he said: 'I don't want to get in wrong with them after all this time. It's years since I did a job and I've got used to not having to worry about the chances of the coppers feeling my collar.'

'Of course, if you've lost your nerve . . . '

'I never lose me nerve, mate.'

'Your skill, perhaps?'

Toby bridled. 'I've kept that all right, never you fear. I bought a safe, a right bastard to open. I practised on that — and others. The new techniques I mean.'

'Then what are you worried about?'

'I don't want to be put down.'

'You won't be. There's another thing — you'll not be robbing a bank in the ordinary sense. Not unless you're getting ideas over and above what I'm asking.'

'If I thought of it I've already forgotten it, mate.'

'You *could* do it and get away with a lot more than five thousand.'

'Yeh, I could — as easy as pie.'

'I don't want that,' said Matt sharply.

'I just told you, I'm not proposing to do it.' Toby flushed the remains of his cigarette down the sink, turned the tap off and said: 'You've been inside this bank, haven't you?'

213

'I had to case the joint, as the Americans say.'

'You must be the fella who tied up the night watchman and scarpered when he got himself untied, then.'

'I tied him in a way that made it possible for him to get free.'

'So's they'd think you made a mucker of the job and got the wind up?' Toby grinned. 'You're smart yourself, Mr. Smith.'

'All I needed to know was the location of the safety deposit section, which I couldn't find out in normal banking hours. I haven't the know-how to open it, so I come to you.' It was all slightly less than the truth because he *had* thought of trying it unaided, at first.

Toby Byass propped his vast backside against the sink and said, with his eyes half-closed: 'I can get in without having to tie-up the watchman.'

'How?'

'He makes a round of the premises. All I need to do is find out where he is at any given time and pick *my* time to get in, see?'

214

'No. You can't open a safety deposit in five minutes while he's in another part of the building. He'll come back and see you.'

'He won't, you know. I already know where he'll be. The watchman is a fella named Wally Bledstowe. Very regular in his habits, takes a little supper break at eleven p.m. on t'dot. He has a cubby-hole of his own where he brews up.'

'How do you know all this?'

'I once thought of doing this particular bank and sort of kept an eye on things. Besides, I know this fella, which is lucky for you. He has this bit of a cubby-hole, so in he goes and the door's on the latch and it swings shut behind him, with a bit of help from me. He always leaves the key on the outside, so I just turn it and there he is stuck while I do the job. That is, if I take this little lot on for you.'

'Are you trying to shake me down for more money?'

'No, five grand is a lot of loot for a simple job. But if I get copped it'll be bad.'

'For both of us, since you'd try to make

things better for yourself by giving me away,' said Matt coolly.

'I'd not hesitate, since I'd be taking the biggest risk.'

'Then I'll make it foolproof for you. When you take the papers from the safety deposit you substitute another lot which I'll give you. Nobody'll even miss anything.'

'You're joking. I've got to get into a strong-room, haven't I?'

'They're not there, my friend. They're ranged in a line outside the strong-room. You won't have to cut your way through three-inch steel doors with a thermic lance — supposing you've got modern equipment like that.'

'I've got one,' said Toby Byass comfortably. 'A beautiful tool it is an' all. Better'n half a dozen oxy-acetylene burners rolled into one.' He detached his bulk from the sink. 'I can't guarantee it without seeing, but I can probably open this deposit without doing any damage.'

'A mark or two,' said Matt, 'but it'll not matter because the strong-room will still be intact and if anybody looks into the safety deposit an envelope will still be *there*.'

Toby Byass opened a cupboard and got out a bottle. 'We'll have a drink on it, then.'

Matt Lancing expelled a long breath through his nose. Everything was working out. Soon there would be only one last thing to do.

He would not flinch from it.

16

It was six o'clock in the evening and they had been on duty since nine that morning and still no sign of going home. Instead, they were all back in the Braxted-Fallon office.

Brooker, catching Bawtry's eye as they went in, made a small gesture with his right hand. Sam grinned, getting the silent message which said, as clearly as if words had been spoken into his private ear, that the Chief Inspector was feelingly aware that the pubs had been open for the last half-hour.

From his padded chair Braxted said without preliminaries: 'We've been on the phone to Hong Kong. Thought you all ought to know the result immediately.'

Brooker leaned forward, no longer even thinking about inroads into his drinking time. Bawtry took a cigarette out, looked at it and put it back. Fallon, for once pipeless, sat back with both hands in the sagging pockets of his permanently rumpled suit.

The Chief Superintendent glanced at a foolscap quarto sheet with scrawled words on it and said: 'I asked the Hong Kong police commissioner to give us any information they have about Leng. They say he was a single man who had worked for several years as an accounts clerk for a firm of exporters and left the colony for England ten days ago, informing his superiors that he was returning here for good.' Braxted peered down at the foolscap again and added: 'The company say he was sober and conscientious and as far as they know lived quietly. No police record.'

'Friends?' Brooker unwrapped another cheroot as he asked the question.

'Very few among his fellow employees but several among the local Chinese, understandably since he was at least partly Chinese himself. He had a small rented flat and kept pretty much to himself. In fact, his whole life in Hong Kong seems to have been virtually without interest, to us certainly.'

Braxted paused. He's got *something* to tell us, Bawtry thought, but he said nothing.

'However, something else has come up.' Braxted looked round and said levelly: 'A month ago the police out there found the body of a man buried under the floorboards of a disused hut in one of the less reputable quarters. More accurately, the remains of a body. The man had been dead at least two years and had been murdered, apparently by strangulation applied with such force that his neck was broken.'

Brooker seemed on the point of speaking, but changed his mind.

The Chief Superintendent said: 'Identity has been established. The clothes contained his passport — Matthew Langley, of 4690 Lei Avenue, Hong Kong.'

Brooker stopped in the act of lighting his cheroot, holding the match while the flame crawled down to his fingers. He dropped the match and said: 'Christ!'

'There could be another Langley, the

name's not entirely uncommon, but the balance of probability is against it.' Braxted looked directly at Bawtry. 'Well, Sam?'

'There doesn't seem to be anything to say, sir — except that we now seem to be up against a completely blank wall. It simply looks as if Leng came to England seeking a man who had already been dead for the last eighteen months.'

'There isn't any doubt about it. The police report that Langley terminated the tenancy of his flat, saying he was going to England. It was assumed that he had done so. In fact, he was murdered at just about that time.'

'Very convenient for the killer, sir.'

'Yes — nobody wondering where he had got to. No awkward questions and eighteen months go by before his body is found, and then only by sheer chance. The hut was struck by lightning and demolition workers moved in and came across the remains.'

'And a year and a half later Leng comes back to Liverpool looking for a fella who no longer exists.' Brooker dragged on his cheroot. 'That leaves us precisely nowhere.'

Bawtry gave up trying to do without a cigarette. 'It doesn't change anything basically. Somebody killed Leng — obviously not Langley, but somebody.'

'Unless he *wasn't* murdered, after all,' said Braxted.

'I still say he was, sir.'

'It's your theory and I backed you up on it, but circumstances can alter cases.'

'Not this one.'

'You're being dogmatic, Sam.'

Bawtry said quietly: 'I'm not trying to justify a cherished belief which has been overtaken by events, sir. Specifically, I'm not merely trying to save my face.'

'I haven't suggested it,' rejoined Braxted sharply.

Fallon looked pointedly at nothing in particular; Brooker watched Bawtry through the cigar haze.

'We've worked on the theory that a man called Langley killed Leng,' said Bawtry slowly. 'The fact that Langley was himself already dead doesn't change the fact that Leng *was* murdered, it simply

222

means we have to look for a different killer. That is, unless we're now going to abandon the theory and accept it that Leng died from a mixture of drink and drugs, self-administered — accidentally or on purpose.'

'I'm taking another look at that possibility,' Braxted said.

'I still believe we have an unsolved murder on our hands, sir.'

'You're playing a hunch, Sam, one of your hunches. I'm not saying they don't come off, some of the time anyway. But it's still a hunch, unsupported by evidence.'

'Leng was looking for someone, he came to Liverpool with that purpose.'

'Leng was looking for Langley, who no longer existed — so who killed Leng?' said Fallon mildly.

Bawtry said: 'Suppose we're on the wrong track altogether — or suppose I am.'

'I don't follow that, Sam.'

'I mean Leng could've been looking for Langley, not knowing he was already dead — and been killed by someone else.'

There was a silence. Braxted ended it. 'You don't sound confident of your own hunch this time.'

'I'm considering possibilities, sir. We can't expect all the answers in two minutes.'

Braxted stood up. 'I'm giving you two weeks. If we don't get something that looks like a solid lead we'll have to close the investigation so far as suspected murder is concerned and . . . ' He broke off as the telephone rang and picked up the receiver. A sudden tight look came on his face.

When he put the instrument down he said: 'Terry Byass escaped from the remand centre a quarter of an hour ago.'

17

The car was parked in a side-street, a five-year-old Morris 1000 with rust pimples starting on the sills. Terry Byass poked his head out of the passage he had dodged into, looked both ways and saw the car only yards away. The key was in the ignition, so the door would be open. Probably only been left for a few minutes.

Footsteps rapped distantly, then a girl rounded the corner of the street, coming his way. A smashing bird, but there was a time for birds and this wasn't it. He took his head back and waited until she had gone past and he could no longer hear her footsteps. He craned his neck forward again. The street was empty. Someone else might come, though. He risked it — almost in a single jump which took him to the car. Sweat was running off him as he slid down in the seat. He turned the ignition key. The purr of the engine was like a murmured reassurance. He stopped sweating. A quick look over his shoulder and he was away, in second to get moving fast.

A minute later he was round the corner and going down Kilshaw Street for the West Derby Road, coming on to it opposite the Grafton Rooms. He remembered going there a week since, looking for crumpet, but it hadn't been his lucky night. He made a left turn, skirting Sheil Park, not too fast; there was no percentage in getting pulled up for speeding. Not that the Jacks would be looking for the Morris yet. Soon, though.

Better ditch it once he was clear of the city and hijack another. Sure to be some lying about, fellas who left their cars outside their homes all night because they couldn't afford a garage or there wasn't space to put one up. On the other hand he mightn't find another car with the key obligingly in the ignition. Press on then, eh? Get down the East Lancs. Road as far as the M6, then thumb a ride north or south, it didn't matter which. It did, though. South was best, down to Birmingham and then on to London.

He'd been down there a few times. Better still, he knew a fella who had a flat, in May Street it was, near the Earls Court Underground station. Snowy Black — what a bloody combination. Good bloke, though, Snowy. 'Any time you feel like switching to The Smoke you're welcome here, Terry' — that was only a month ago. Right, mate, I'm taking you up on it. Make a good team, him and Snowy. A partnership. Loot Unlimited. Just the job.

He got out on to the eastbound dual carriageway, keeping to the inside lane all the way to the M6. Still no coppers around. Why bother to hitch a ride? Might be stuck at the motorway interchange for ages, waiting. Motorists increasingly shied at giving lifts, you never knew what you might be letting yourself in for these days. He drove up the sliproad and down on to the motorway, crossing into the middle lane and treading hard down on the pedal.

Fifty-five, sixty, sixty-eight. Going like a bomb. Hold it just under the seventy limit, that'll be fine. A bloody great Merc showed up behind, flashing headlamps at him. Get in the fast lane, I'm not shifting over for you. The Mercedes switched lanes and streaked past. Must be doing ninety. I should've got me a Merc; happen I'll even buy one when I get weaving down in London.

He looked dartingly at the polythene bag he had dumped in the other seat, stuffed with rings, watches, brooches. Worth plenty, that little lot. He'd seen some of the price tags on them when he walked into the shop off Hardisty Street just before it closed and less than half an hour after he gave them the slip at the remand centre. One old fella and a girl in charge. He'd terrorised them with a stolen knife at the Judy's throat, then made her load up the bag while he stood over her and the old fella trembled like a jelly on a plate. After that he'd bundled them into that bit of an office at the back and locked the door on them, first ripping out the telephone. Easy.

Then he'd sneaked into his own old fella's house and nicked that thermic lance he'd always fancied. Come in useful, that. And now I'm on me way to

London town with a few thousand nicker in loot, buying me way in. I'll cut you in sixty-forty, Snowy, how about that? Snowy'd fence the stuff, he knew that. Everything's great, it is great. Better not risk driving this heap all the way, though. Get as far as Wolverhampton, leave the car and catch a train to Brum, then another to London. That's it.

Signs loomed as the miles sped past. Knutsford, Middlewich, Sandbach. I'm doing all right. I know what, I'll come off at Dunston, leave the car somewhere near the Gailey roundabout and get a bus into Wolverhampton.

Newcastle-under-Lyme, Stone, Stafford — we're nearly there, Terry me boyo. He slammed the pedal hard down to the floorboards, watching the needle shoot up to seventy-three. Flat out, won't do any more.

He laughed, loud above the whine from the engine. His hands were firm on the steering wheel. Then, without warning, he no longer had control. The car sagged to the right, lurched madly sideways. The right offside tyre was a blowout and the car thudded across the central reservation, full tilt into a four-litre Jag pelting up the northbound carriageway.

★ ★ ★

An inspector and a couple of detective sergeants were investigating the jewellery shop raid, trying to extract a coherent picture from an old chap in a state of shock and a teenage girl only a twitch away from outright hysteria.

Dan Aiken, the inspector, said: 'We're not getting much. The boss'll have something to say if we can't do better'n this.'

One of the plainclothes men grinned faintly. 'He's still away, isn't he?'

'Aye, on the 7th Senior Command course, but he'll be back tomorrow and expecting results from us.'

'All we've got is that a young bastard walked in, held them up with a knife and made the young lady fill a polythene bag with valuables. Could be anybody — and no dabs because he didn't touch anything himself.'

'We'll try again . . . ' Aiken paused. The girl had stopped shaking. 'Yes, miss?'

'I remember one thing, sir — he had ginger hair.'

'A redheaded villain . . . ' Aiken fingered his magnificent moustaches. 'I wonder!'

The other detective said: 'What?'

'Terry Byass broke out from the remand centre and he's got flaming hair. Contact Headquarters and get them to put out a general alert — one thing's for sure, he'll be out of 'G' Division by now.'

Jenny Mycroft had radioed the call when a message came through from the North Staffs police: *Morris 1000 with Liverpool registration in collision with Jaguar on M6 after crossing central reservation. Driver of Morris has license in name of Terence James Byass, 17 Santon Street, Liverpool. In hospital with compound fracture left arm, fractured pelvis, multiple cuts and abrasions, but expected to live. Driver of Jaguar thrown clear, escaped with broken wrist and minor lacerations. Polythene bag found in Morris contained rings, watches and other jewellery, value not yet assessed. Also found, one thermic lance.*

Brooker mouthed the terse words, then said: 'Terry Byass couldn't use a thermic lance if he tried, but his old fella could. Only he didn't raid the shop and he wasn't in the car.'

'There'll be dabs on the lance,' mused Bawtry. 'We can ask North Staffs to put them on the telephoto. Not that it implicates Toby.'

'Happen not in this particular case, but possessing that tool could suggest felonious intent. He might've run through his money and be getting ready to start up again.'

'It's possible, but in that case what was Terry doing with the thing?'

'You're asking *me*?'

'It was sort of a general question,' grinned Bawtry. 'What do you want me to do — see Toby again?'

'Might be worth a quick visit.'

'I'm still on the murder investigation.'

'If there still is one. Braxted seems doubtful.'

'What about you?'

'I'm on your side,' Brooker replied. 'But that's not to say you can't take an hour off to chat up Toby Byass. Nobody to touch you at the old interrogation.'

'I sometimes wish I didn't have that reputation, it just lands me in more work.'

'That's right — and you love it,' said Brooker cheerfully.

When Bawtry got to the terrace house he literally dead-heated with Toby Byass, in the act of putting the front door key in the lock.

'What, you again, Mr. B.?'

'I've something to tell you, Toby.'

The fat man eyed him sideways. 'Something about what?'

'Your lad, for one thing.'

'What's he done now? I thought he was in custody. Well, come in.'

They went inside. Toby listened and said: 'About all he's fit for, waving a knife about and smashing-up a stolen car.'

'Happen this'll be a lesson to him.'

'I hope so, but I doubt it. I suppose I'd better go and see him.'

'Up to you, Toby. There's something else.'

'I thought there might be.'

'The police found a thermic lance in the car.' Bawtry watched as he spoke, but Toby's face was as bland as the moon it resembled.

'A thermic lance is an acutely efficient cutting instrument known to be favoured by the more technically expert among safe-breakers,' Bawtry went on. 'Not that I need to instruct you in the finer points of your profession.'

'My late profession, Mr. B., I'll thank you to remember that,' said Toby with monumental dignity. 'You've no call to come here casting nasturtiums, as they say.'

'Aspersions.'

'It was just a joke. What's Terry having this lance got to do with me?'

'I'll not beat about the bush, Toby. *Is* it yours?'

Toby Byass took a ready-rolled cigarette from a two-ounce tobacco tin and lit it with a hand that was not quite steady. Bawtry thought: it could be a whisky tremble — or something else. Happen I'll find out. Or not.

The silence was as tense as stretched elastic. Then, like a man who finally makes up his mind, Toby waddled to a cupboard, went down on one gross knee and peered inside. When he straightened-up he said: 'All right, it's mine. I didn't know it had gone. He must've come in while me back was turned, the young bastard. But I've never used it, not on a job — straight up, Mr. B.'

'What did you want with it then?'

'I just fancied having one. I got it a year or two since, I wanted to see how it worked. I've used it, sure, but only here at home. I'll show you.' He led the way into the parlour and aimed a finger at a safe in the dark corner. 'I used it on that. Yeh, it works all right, marvellous. But I've never done a proper job with it. I've quit, like I said.'

'You're a fool to hang on to a thing like that, then.'

'I was meaning to chuck it out, but I kept putting it off, you know how it is.' Toby's gaze went to the old-fashioned clock on the mantelpiece. The hands showed 7.37. 'Look, I'm telling you the truth, what more do you want?'

'Nothing just now.'

'What's just now mean?'

'What it says.'

'I'm not planning to use the bloody lance — any road, I haven't even got it now, so what's all the fuss about?' Toby dragged on the remains of his cigarette, trying not to look at the clock again.

He's got the fidgets, he came back for a wash or a shave or something and he's expecting something or he wants to go out and I'm in the way, thought Bawtry.

Aloud, he said: 'It was just the lance, we wanted to know about it.'

'Well, I've told you, I can't do no more than that, can I?'

'That's right, you can't.' Bawtry swung his hat. 'Well, I'll be going.'

The relief on the fat face was unmistakable. So there *was* something. But Bawtry had no idea what it could be and no reason for staying. He was going towards the door when he said affably: 'I see you're on the phone now.'

Toby started, then said with a shrug:

'Had it put in yest'day.' He grinned. 'Useful for ringing me bookie.'

Bawtry was in the act of closing the street door behind him when the instrument rang. He left the door barely an inch off the latch and listened.

The wheezing voice just reached him. 'I'll be a bit late. Sorry, something held me up. In half an hour at t'Green Acres. In the lounge, right.'

Bawtry synchronised closing the door with the sound of the receiver going down on the rest with a bang and went out to his car. The Green Acres was a pub off Brownlow Hill within sight of the vast spread of the Roman Catholic Cathedral. He drove there, parked on a demolition site behind the pub and sat in the car trying to extract something from his thoughts, but all that surfaced was the feeling that Toby Byass was seeing somebody about something that might or might not bear investigation. Do no harm to take a look. He walked unhurriedly round to the pub.

The lounge was long, running from the front to the back of the place, with the bar counter occupying almost the entire length. There were about a couple of dozen customers in. Bawtry ordered a tonic water with ice and lemon and took it to a table set against the facing wall and opened the *Liverpool Echo*; the full-sized pages, spread out, would do as a cover when Toby Byass showed up.

Meanwhile, he let his eyes take in the room. No villains on hand, anyway. Over to the right a middle-aged man in a grey suit was holding forth to a couple of cronies about what the Government ought to do if it wanted to retain the confidence reposed in it at the last election. To the left a burly fellow was chatting-up one of the three barmaids, a splendidly constructed one with hair like a yellow bird-cage. Several other men were at the bar and the rest of the transient male population was dotted round the room, making an undertow of indistinguishable conversation.

No sign yet of Toby Byass. He ought to be here by now if he was keeping his appointment. Bawtry tried to pick out the man Toby was supposed to meet, without success. It could be any one of the two dozen. A tall man in a beautifully-tailored blue suit and polished black Oxfords came through the open door, crossed to the bar, bought a small whisky and sat alone at a table half-way down the room.

More time passed. Bawtry looked at his watch. Forty-three minutes since the telephone call. A waiter drifted up, asked the newcomer if he wanted another, got a head-shake in return and made his way to Bawtry, who ordered another Indian tonic water.

There was something wrong, there had to be. Perhaps Toby had fallen under a bus, thought Bawtry, not seriously. Other men were coming in from the street, the whole place was filling up. The man in the dark blue suit rose abruptly and started along the room, heading for the door. His lips were slightly pursed and as he went past Bawtry heard the subdued hum-ming.

It was the *Merry Widow* waltz . . .

Well, a lot of people hummed to themselves. Yes, but they didn't all hum that particular melodic line. Just a

239

coincidence. Maybe. The man went out and Bawtry rose no less abruptly, missing his reflection in the wide wall mirror behind the bar counter.

Four men were jostling through the door and Bawtry nearly cannoned into them. One was saying something about a demo approaching down Brownlow Hill — 'Bloody hippies, they want destroying!'

Outside the pub Bawtry could see the humming man in the distance, walking quickly. He went after him without any clear idea of what he was going to do. For God's sake, you can't arrest a fella for humming the *Merry Widow*. No, but it was odd — too much of a coincidence. Worth tailing him. See where he goes, take it from there, eh?

Bawtry was lengthening his stride when he heard the confusion of sound ahead. When he reached Brownlow Hill the road was jammed with demonstrators marching abreast with banners he hadn't the time to read. The man ahead had already stepped off the pavement, weaving in and out on his way to the other side of the road. Suddenly, the leading ranks broke, for no apparent reason. The pressure behind mounted and the front section spread in a scattered line.

By the time Bawtry fought his way through the press of bodies the humming man had vanished.

18

'Tiger' Brooker was still at Headquarters, in the big detectives' room, though a light whisky breath announced the fact that he hadn't been there all the time.

'Anything, Sam?'

'Yes and no.' Bawtry sat on the edge of a desk and explained briefly.

Brooker jingled coins in his trouser pocket, a recurring habit which Bawtry found vaguely irritating, though he kept the fact to himself. 'Pity you lost this fella, Sam.'

'Yes, if the procession hadn't broken ranks I'd have kept him in sight.'

Brooker's voice blared: 'Bloody demonstrators, I'm sick of hearing about them.'

'They claim they're exercising the right to dissent in a democratic society.'

'The sods don't give a damn about a democratic society. Most of them are out to smash it, you know that. And what are they going to shove in its place?'

'A lot of them don't seem to know.'

'Some of them know all right — a revolutionary dictatorship erected on the ruins of the very system which gives them the freedom they'd deny to everyone else, the bastards.' Brooker grinned and went on: 'Happen it was just coincidence, this fella humming, though.'

'It's possible, but the fact that it was the same tune is odd.'

'Toby Byass,' mused Brooker. 'He could've been delayed and turned up after you left. You're sure there weren't any known villains in that boozer?'

'I didn't see any. Perhaps Toby was simply going to see a respectable friend. After all, he's been clean for years.'

'You don't think he could've been meeting this humming fella, do you?'

Bawtry nursed his powerful jaw. 'I ought to have considered that. On the other hand, if that was the idea why didn't he turn up?'

'There *is* that,' agreed Brooker. He blew out a stream of aromatic smoke. 'God Almighty, we're getting precisely nowhere, either with the murder or the bank job. The Chief Con is starting to get restive.'

'Why, have you see him?'

'No, but Braxted had a five-minute interview. He says the old man wants evidence to substantiate the murder theory and wants it quick.'

'I thought I was being given two weeks.'

'You *had* two weeks. The Chief Con thinks it's too long.'

'What's his idea of a time limit?'

'He didn't specify, but he probably means days instead of weeks.'

'Are you still with me on this?'

'Yes. Mind you,' said Brooker coolly, 'I still think you're playing a hunch, but with you they have a way of coming off.'

'Not every time.'

'Well, you can't win 'em all and you may be wrong with this one, but I'm taking a chance the other way. Any point in seeing Toby Byass again?'

'I doubt it. Even if he's leaving the straight and narrow he'll not cough anything.'

'You're probably right. Besides, it's not Toby we're after. Somehow, we've *got* to get a lead on the Leng murder.'

'I could go back to the pub where Terry Byass ran into Leng and see if I can trace anyone else he may have spoken to.'

'It's a bit thin, but it might be worth a try.' Brooker put his cheroot down and said: 'By the way, I dropped in on Ben Hodson. He thought you'd like to know they caught Whitey Malley before he could start going through Biddy McShann's brass.'

'Good.'

'Oh, while I remember, Alison Raynes. She's home and sends you her love.'

'*Does* she?'

'Yes, better not tell Carol.'

'She wouldn't mind.'

'Meaning she can be sure of you, which I don't doubt. You've a great girl there, Sam.'

'She likes *you*,' said Bawtry.

Brooker's hard, lined face lightened. 'You're not joking?'

'No.'

'Does she know about Marion?'

Bawtry nodded.

'Did you tell her?'

'Not for a long time, then it got into the conversation one night.' Bawtry felt slightly uncomfortable.

But Brooker merely said: 'That's all right, Sam. Naturally you told her. Most of the fellas on the strength talk about my wife running out on me, behind my back I mean.'

'I haven't.'

'It wouldn't worry me if you had. You can't stop people talking about a thing like that.'

Bawtry hesitated, then said: 'You've never heard from Marion?'

'No. It doesn't matter, it's all over and done with. If she'd come home in the first weeks or even months I'd have taken her back. Not now, though. I've got over it. Well, happen not properly, you never do, but enough not to want to try again. She's made her bed, and she can lie on it. I hope it gives her a crick in the back.'

A thought came unbidden into Bawtry's mind. As if in answer to it, Brooker said: 'Sometimes I fancy a woman, I'm not past it yet.'

Still Bawtry said nothing and Brooker went on: 'After Laura got killed in that smash-up on the East Lancs Road you lived for years without, didn't you?'

'Once in four years and then I felt guilty, somehow.'

'That's bloody daft, Sam.'

'I suppose it is, but that's how I felt.'

'Well, nobody'd call me a ladies' man, that's probably one of my troubles, but I haven't gone without, not altogether.' Brooker straightened his tie absently and said: 'A widow, ten years younger than me. Just now and again. I oblige her — or she obliges me. She doesn't want to remarry and I can't, anyway, I'm not divorced. Sort of a handy arrangement.'

The unexpected revelation made Bawtry uncomfortable again. Somehow he had never imagined Brooker confiding a situation like that; in fact, he had never imagined Brooker making love to a woman, not even to Marion. It was ridiculous, of course, but he simply hadn't visualised it.

Brooker said with a chuckle: 'Now I'll tell *you* something: I feel as guilty as hell every time I visit Joyce. How about a drink?'

'All right.'

'Just a quickie, then off you go to that lass of yours. We'll nip round to Sam's Bar — appropriate.'

Two half-pints of bitter later Bawtry went home to Carol. 'You've been in the pub,' she said when he kissed her. 'With the Chief Inspector?'

'How did you guess?'

'You've become friends as well as colleagues lately.'

'You like Brooker, don't you?'

'Yes, I do. Under that hard front there's a very likeable man struggling to get out.'

Sam grinned. 'I'll have to tell him that.'

'Don't you dare tell Mr. Brooker I've been talking about him!'

'He wouldn't mind, he thinks you're a great girl.'

'Well, that's nice.'

'It's nothing to what I think,' said Sam, reaching for her.

Carol laughed, dodging away. 'You're not going to chase me round the kitchen, surely?'

'Why not? It's as good a place as any.'

'It isn't, you know.'

'Well, no time like the present then . . . '

'You eat your nice supper,' said Carol austerely.

'Feed the brute first, eh?'

'You're not brutish, you're the nicest man I ever met.'

'Even if I am only three years off fifty?'

'I wouldn't care if you were three years off ninety.'

'By God, I would. We both would.'

They were sitting at the table when Carol said: 'What's Mr. Brooker's first name?'

'Esmond.'

'You're joking!'

'No, that's his name, though hardly anybody on the strength knows it. He'd have forty-five fits if he even thought anybody knew.'

'It certainly doesn't suit him. What do you call him?'

'Come to think of it, I never call him anything.'

'The men call him 'Tiger' Brooker, don't they?'

'Sometimes — when he's not present.'

'Is he tigerish?'

'He can be when he wants. With some of the villains, particularly.'

'How's the case coming along, or shouldn't I pry?'

'I don't mind.'

'It's a sort of tradition that policemen don't discuss their work, even with their wives, isn't it?'

'Yes, but it's different somehow with you. As to the case, it's not coming along too well — in fact, hardly at all.'

'It will do, Sam.'

'I wish I had your simple faith in my infallibility.'

'I dare say you make mistakes, but you have a way of getting there in the end.'

'Just at the moment I can't even see a glimmering of the end.'

Carol poured coffee and said thoughtfully: 'I didn't get to know anything from the young housemen. Incidentally, there's something funny about all this, I mean about it going back to Hong Kong.'

'Not really, Leng came here to look up someone he'd known out there.'

'I don't mean that, I mean it's funny about this unknown man Langley being murdered in Hong Kong.'

Bawtry put his cup down. 'I've thought about that, but so far as Leng's death is concerned there's no connection. Langley died ages ago — well, getting on for a couple of years, if not more.'

'I still think it's odd, Sam.'

'How can an old murder in Hong Kong have anything to do with one that's only just happened thousands of miles away?'

Carol sighed. 'I don't know, but it's very odd. Oh, well, you'll get to the bottom of everything, you usually do. Now you can help me wash-up and we'll watch the telly.'

'Why, is there something you want to see?'

'*The Untouchables*.'

Bawtry grinned. 'I think you fancy Elliot Ness.'

'Well, he's a bit like you, quiet and determined.'

'I'm determined on one thing before the night's out.'

'I thought you might be. Well, I won't be untouchable — later.'

It was later still when Bawtry suddenly sat up in bed. Carol stirred and said: 'What's the matter, Sam?'

'Nothing, you go back to sleep, love.'

She put her head on his shoulder and he slid down with his right arm round her. Something she had said, hours before, had risen in his mind. About it being odd that an unknown man named Langley had been murdered all that time ago in a far-off spot that was just a place on the map. But it couldn't have anything to do with a murder in Liverpool nearly two years later. All Carol had said was that it was funny. Why should he remember that in the middle of the night? He didn't know. But the recollected words fired a new trend of thought. It's daft, you're letting your imagination run away with you, like a writer waking suddenly in the small hours with a startling idea and when daylight comes he knows that's all it is, just a startling idea that won't work out.

But when he strode into Headquarters for the morning conference Bawtry still had the thought and it wasn't crazy.

19

Brilliant sunshine poured through the side window in a vast wedge, a million tiny dust particles shimmering in it. Braxted, who was sitting directly in line, got up and drew a Venetian blind. He went back to his seat behind the desk and sat there drumming the fingers of both hands on its unlittered surface.

'You've no shred of proof, of course, Bawtry.' The use of the surname meant that Braxted was savouring the theory and not caring much for the taste.

Bawtry felt himself stiffening, but he went on levelly: 'I'm not stating a case, sir. I'm doing no more than put a possibility up for discussion.'

'Your wife makes a comment and in the middle of the night it starts that nimble brain of yours working.' It was Fallon who spoke, charging his noisome pipe.

'I just had this sudden thought while I

was turning over what she said. I thought it'd look wildly far-fetched in the morning, Ted — but it doesn't. Well, not to me.'

Brooker, leaning off the edge of his chair with his hands dangling between his knees, said: 'Nor me.'

'It's all theorising, with nothing to back it up,' Braxted objected. 'You're asking us to believe that a man murdered eighteen months ago in Hong Kong and recently identified as Matthew Langley is someone entirely different?'

'I'm not saying it as a proven fact, sir. I'd like us to look at it as a possibility, that's all.'

'If the man murdered in Hong Kong was identified as Langley why should Leng come here looking for him?'

Bawtry didn't answer directly. He shifted his bulk and said: 'We've had cases before where something was right under our noses and we didn't immediately see it.'

'Well?'

'It's a long way from Hong Kong to Pitt Street — but that's the connection which interests me, sir. It's too coincidental.'

'Why, if Leng didn't know Langley was already dead?'

'I'm looking at the possibility that Leng knew about the body identified out there as Langley. I also think that in some way he found out or guessed that this dead man *wasn't* Langley.'

'Then why did he drop the name in conversation with Li Chou?'

'Happen he didn't want to bandy the other one about in public,' Brooker said slowly.

Bawtry nodded. 'He could have discovered that Langley was living here in Liverpool under another name — the name he assumed when he switched identities with the man whose body has lately been found in Hong Kong, and then solely by chance.'

'*How* did he know all this?'

'I can't answer that, sir, but I think that somehow he did — and if I'm right it explains everything. Specifically, it explains why Leng himself was murdered — it gives us the clear motive.'

'You're saying that a man named Langley, wrongly supposed to have been killed in Hong Kong, is here in Liverpool using another man's name — the name of the man he killed out there. Why?'

'Loot,' said Brooker laconically.

'That's an assumption which doesn't take us any nearer.'

'Happen it will if we worry it like a pack of ferrets, sir.'

Bawtry lit a cigarette and said: 'The body found in Hong Kong was beyond recognition. The identity was presumed from papers found on it and a stitched label in the clothing. The police there say no relative came forward. They think the man was a transient.'

'No shortage of fellas like that out there, I imagine,' remarked Fallon.

'One other point — if Langley isn't here under a dead man's name it's difficult to see why Leng was murdered, since Langley was the man he was seeking.'

'It's far-fetched,' said Braxted. He pushed his shoulders up the padded back of his chair. 'We've still nothing positive to go on.' A thin smile touched one corner of his mouth. 'Just one of Sam's hunches . . . but it could be right.'

Bawtry went out. It was another day in the brilliant Indian summer, the streets thronged with strollers and shoppers, not a care in the world. No, that wasn't right. There'd be plenty with gnawing private anxieties if you whisked away the masks and saw the frightened realities behind a hundred brave fronts.

Somewhere in the city, happen in this very street, was a frightened man with murder on his conscience, if he had one. Or a man without conscience, only the chill fear of discovery. Perhaps not even that; instead, a man who had killed twice without compunction, a man warmed by the conviction that he could never be found out. That's what they all thought, though, wasn't it? The almost pathological egotism of the killer who planned every last microscopic move. But always there was a chink in the pattern, if you looked hard enough and often enough. The trouble was knowing where to start looking.

The thoughts chased each other through Bawtry's mind as he walked up Church Street. Walking alone was something he liked to do when a case got difficult; you could think without the distraction of conversation. It wasn't going to take him straight through to a conclusion, he knew that, but it helped to think uninterruptedly, laying out facts in your mind and allowing thoughts to shape themselves.

He reached the intersection where Paradise Street runs into Whitechapel and walked on up Lord Street, going towards the Pierhead. He was crossing St. George's Crescent when he noticed the woman behind the wheel of a car halted in the traffic. Della Lancing half-turned and smiled in recognition, lifting a gloved hand.

Bawtry returned the smile and the car moved on. Suddenly, for no reason apart from having seen her, he remembered the odd tone in her voice when they last met — the odd way she had said yes when he asked if she was on her way home at the time of the accident. Well, there was nothing odd about her now, just a nice smile because she had recalled him. Wonder what that odd tone *was* about, though.

A thought came to him. He shrugged. It was nothing to do with murder. Keep your eye on the ball, chum. He walked on.

★   ★   ★

Della Lancing left the car at a parking meter and went into a restaurant off Hanover Street, one she had never used before because she didn't want to run into anyone who knew her. Like Bawtry, she wanted to think without interruption.

She was worried. There was something wrong with Matt, she had sensed it half a dozen times in as many days. Of course, he might simply be disturbed because he had caught her out; but she felt intuitively that it wasn't that. Well, she still had the whip hand over him, hadn't she? Perhaps that was it — the frustration of knowing that he had to put up with whatever she chose to do.

No, it wasn't that, either. It was something else, she was sure of it, something that was going on inside his mind. He was up to something. But what? He couldn't divorce her, couldn't even leave her unless she consented and she didn't want a separation, legal or otherwise. She liked being Mrs. Matthew Lancing — the fine house, the entertaining, all the rest of it. Anyway, he hadn't suggested a separation, legal or otherwise. He hadn't suggested anything. In fact, she was scarcely seeing him just now except at breakfast. Four nights on the run he hadn't even returned for dinner, ringing up to plead business.

There's something going on, for God's sake I've got to find out what it is. I don't love him, I probably never did, but I liked being married to him when things were all right between us. If he's fiddling about with the firm's money that could be it, that and fear of discovery, our whole lovely way of life smashed. That'd be bad enough, but there's something else, I can sense it. I can't go on living in this atmosphere, exchanging brittle meaningless conversations on the rare occasions when we have any conversation. He's not even sleeping with me. Well, I asked for that, didn't I? Besides, I don't give a damn. But he's up to something, I know he is. Somehow, I've got to find out what it is.

She paid her small bill and went out to the car. Nearly six o'clock. If she hurried she could just reach the office before all the staff left. Matt wouldn't be there, he'd gone to London and wouldn't be back until the next day.

Della drove on to the private parking ground behind the office block and went up in the lift. The pert blonde in the reception foyer looked up inquiringly. Nice little piece, wonder if he's doing something there? Probably not. Suppose he's gone queer? God, what a thought, married to a homo. The very existence of them made her feel ill, they ought to be destroyed. A little of what you fancy, strictly orthodox, that's one thing; but the other — ugh!

She swept the passing thoughts from her mind and said: 'I've just called in for something — perhaps you'll tell Mr. Fairfax I'm here?'

The girl spoke into an intercom and old Fairfax came bustling in. Well, perhaps not all that old or he'd have been retired, but looking old with his bifocals and that shiny out-of-style suit, wide trousers with turn-ups — though weren't they supposed to be on the way in again?

Della gave him one of her dazzling smiles. 'Mr. Lancing left a small parcel for me in his office, I've dropped in to pick it up.'

The chief clerk blinked. 'You're just in time, then. In a few more minutes we'd all have gone, Mrs. Lancing.'

'Yes, I forgot about it earlier. I'll go in and collect it, shall I?'

'Of course.' He led the way. Della thought: he'll probably tell Matt I've been in. Well, I don't care if he does. I'll have a showdown, that's all. On the other hand, he might not bother to mention it.

Fairfax opened the door to Matt's office and stood deferentially to one side. 'I don't recall Mr. Lancing leaving a parcel . . . '

'He said it would be in one of the desk drawers.'

'Ah, that explains it.'

She walked into the room, half-turned and said winningly: 'I'll let myself out, Mr. Fairfax — I expect you want to finish off your work for the day. I'll not be more than a few moments.'

'Well, there are one or two little things I want to . . . ' He smiled at her and went away.

Della looked round the room. It was the first time she had been in it, though not the first time in the building. So this is where the big shot makes all those vital policy decisions, is it? Matt Lancing, chairman and managing director. What the hell *is* he up to?

She went back and closed the door softly, then stood in the middle of the fitted red carpet, taking it all in. Does himself well, nothing but the best. But where do I look and, more pertinently, what am I looking for? I don't know, it's just a feeling that there might be something, anything, I don't know exactly what.

After a moment she stood behind the polished executive desk with its leather-bound embossed blotter, dove grey telephones, crimson annunicator-box and pastel-tinted angle light. The desk drawers were unlocked. She slid them out, two at a time. Note-pads, pens, miscellaneous office stuff; a box of cigars, nearly full, Ramon Allones. Several letters marked *Personal*. She glanced at the contents, but they meant nothing, just business communications.

To the right of the desk and ranged against one of the walls was a line of dove grey filing cabinets, also unlocked. She riffled through them with little interest and no result. A safe stood in a corner, mounted on a concrete base tricked-out to look like marble. It was locked. Well, what else did you expect, Della? If he *has* anything secret he'd not leave it lying around out in the open, for goodness sake. No, but I thought perhaps there might be something, perhaps some small thing that would give me a hint about what's going on in that scheming head of his. Well, there isn't, see?

I've been a fool to come here, what the hell did I expect to find, anyway? I still don't know. Something, though. Anyway, I couldn't resist coming. Might as well pack it in, I suppose. Damn! I know one thing, I wouldn't mind a drink, just a quick one on the house. Well, he's had a nice little bar installed. Think of everything, don't you, my darling husband?

She went behind the bar, reached for a bottle of *Antiquary* and looked for an optic measure. It was on the shelf below the polished bar top. So was something else, a square-shaped bottle about half-full of tablets.

Della picked it up. There was no label on the bottle, nothing to indicate what the tablets were. A funny sensation stirred in her, funny peculiar. Footsteps sounded in the passage beyond the room and for a second cold panic swept through her. The footsteps went away. She could hear herself breathing, jaggedly. Matt's not come back, he's in London; just the same, better get out of here. What's in that bottle though, and what's it doing under the bar?

She tilted the bottle and let one of the tablets slide into her palm. There was a way to find out . . .

★   ★   ★

Matt Lancing had concluded his business in London. It would be the last deal he made for the company. There was only one more thing to do and Toby Byass would be doing it. He had fixed it after leaving that pub when Toby failed to turn up; or, rather, he *had* turned up but had pulled back when he spotted that detective inspector's reflection in the wall mirror behind the bar. Smart.

'Sam bloody Bawtry it was,' Toby had said. 'Just dropped in for a drink, I reckon — but I didn't want him to see me with you, boss.'

For a few minutes Matt had felt uneasy. What was it that fellow had said down in London — something about Sam Bawtry being a dangerous man if you ever got on the wrong side of the law. But Bawtry couldn't know what was being planned, it was totally impossible for anybody even to guess. Just a coincidence his being in that bar lounge. The uneasiness ebbed and died. Matt felt buoyant, confident of the final outcome.

Everything was going to be all right. Besides, he had an alibi, hadn't he? Two hundred miles away in London, dining with the top brass of International Exporters Ltd., finally returning to his hotel, making sure he exchanged good-night words with the head porter — then sliding out unobserved to catch a late plane for Speke and the last hand in the game. No, there was to be one more.

The last trick and he would take it . . .

20

Bawtry was at Princes Landing Stage, looking out across the broad sweep of the river. The three crowded decades which had gone since he came to Liverpool from the village where he was born up on the Fylde coast had never dimmed the fascination which the sight and sound of the waterfront first stirred in him. Down the years it had become part of him, the river and the city he loved and would never leave, not even when retirement was forced on him ... and that was something he didn't care to contemplate.

He turned away and started back for Headquarters, not consciously struggling with the case now, just letting thoughts surface. They drifted into his mind of their own volition, scattering and nudging one another. They made a right jumble, he thought wryly. A handsome sophisticated woman with an odd inflexion in her voice who had knocked down Alison

Raynes and unwittingly reshaped her life for the better; a man named Leng murdered by a man named Langley whom he had come half across the world to contact; another man lying dead for eighteen months under the floor-boards of a hovel in Hong Kong; an ex-safe blower in touch with a humming man who had made an odd kind of raid on a bank; Terry Byass mangled in a motorway crash. What did any of these things have in common one with the other?

But they had all happened round about the same time, within days. It didn't necessarily mean anything, though, why should it? Just the same, the recollections kept impinging on him, he could not get rid of them. For Pete's sake, stop it — all you have to do is find the man Leng came from Hong Kong to see. As simple as that, like bloody hell it was simple.

With an effort Bawtry swept everything except the murder from his mind. But only moments later it was all back, a warring montage of seemingly disparate events. Why hadn't Toby Byass turned up at the Green Acres? That was funny, too.

Well, go and ask him, then. As if that would do any good; if Toby had anything to hide he'd keep it hidden. But he'd know the identity of the man who hummed to himself. Suppose they're up to something together? Better to catch them at it, eh? Have a couple of d-c's keep watch. All right, I'll fix it. Meanwhile, I'd better concentrate on murder.

He was at this point in his meditations when he reached Waterloo Place and almost walked slap into Bill Crawfurd as he stepped out of a shop doorway. Crawfurd, a tall rangily-built man about Bawtry's own age, was an expatriate Scot who had been on Merseyside since he left Perth in his late teens to join the reporting staff of one of the local weeklies, moving to evening paper work as a sub-editor, then going back on the outside as a Liverpool staffer for one of the nationals. He was a bachelor living in a flat up near the university campus, a tireless operator who drank consistently without either putting on weight or losing his grip. Like Bawtry, he had a deep-rooted affection for the city. He also had a vast storehouse of Merseyside stories, some unprintable, and an encyclopaedic knowledge of what went on in front of and behind the scenes.

'Hello, Sam — nice bumping into you.' Crawfurd's accent still had its original Scottish burr, but after many years of alien residence it had become impregnated with the characteristic Liverpool inflexions; the combined effect gave his voice a curiously compelling impact.

Bawtry grinned. 'It's a moot point who bumped into who — or is it whom? My fault. I was walking in a bit of a day-dream, I'm afraid.'

'What you want then is Auntie Maggie's remedy.'

'Or old Doc Crawfurd's?'

'Aye, a breath of the Highland heather, taken in liquid form, will do you what they call a power of good.'

'All right, just one.'

They walked on and were going through the doors into the Green Acres when Bawtry suddenly stopped, looking straight ahead at the wall mirror behind the long bar.

'Seen a ghost?' asked Crawfurd.

'Just something I ought to have noticed before, the fact that the mirror over there gives a panoramic view of the room as you enter.' They stood at the bar and Bawtry explained.

'You think Toby Byass spotted you as he came in and went straight out?'

Bawtry nodded and the reporter said casually: 'If it's not a leading question — or even if it is — does this have anything to do with the Pitt Street business?'

'Nothing, so far as I know.'

'You just think Toby might be returning to his old pursuits, is that it?'

'I don't know that, either,' answered Bawtry equably. 'I was merely wondering, that's all.'

'I see Toby around, mostly in pubs. I can tell you one thing, he doesn't hang out with any of the local villains.'

'Well, he never did. A loner is our Toby. As a matter of fact, we've nothing whatever against him.'

Crawfurd said directly: 'I've been doing a bit of thinking about Leng. He was stabbed but actually died of an overdose of drink and drugs, that much emerged at the inquest. Are you by any chance suggesting that the dose wasn't self-administered?'

'I'm not suggesting, Bill, and I'll thank you not to write a story saying anything different.'

'That means you *are* suggesting it.' Crawfurd sipped whisky and added: 'All right, I'll play along. Keep well in with the police — primary rule for newspaper-men.'

'You don't always observe it.'

'This time, anyway. And if I hear anything on my rounds you get the information first.'

'Thanks.' Bawtry pondered for a moment. Then he said: 'You and Jim Copley know more about what goes on in this city than most people. I don't mean more about actual crime, that's our business and we're as well informed as it's possible to be, but more about the ins and outs of local life.'

The journalist said nothing and Bawtry went on: 'We have reason to believe that

Leng was looking for a man named Langley who came here from Hong Kong. We've checked on all persons with this name, but none of them fits.'

'You think this man killed Leng, is that it?'

'We think he may be able to assist us in our inquiries,' answered Bawtry, poker-faced.

The newspaperman shrugged. 'I shouldn't have said that, I suppose.'

'I can't stop you saying anything you like, Bill.'

'And do I know such a man, you are about to ask.' Crawfurd's face puckered. 'In a seaport like this there's probably more than a few men who've been in Hong Kong, but I don't know of them personally.'

'It was just a shot in the dark, a chance that you might know something. A man named Langley, perhaps living in digs or under cover and almost certainly using a different name.'

'The Hong Kong connection seems to be the key,' said Crawfurd. 'Tell you what, I'll have a word with Dick Halloran. He specialises in foreign stories with a Liverpool slant and might just conceivably have heard something that connects.'

'No harm in asking him,' replied Bawtry mechanically. It didn't seem promising, but anything was worth a try.

He went back to Headquarters and was going through the main office when he saw Bert Collins leaning against the counter talking to Joe Oldfield.

'Well, I'm here again, back on't treadmill.'

'You've got a right tan — where've you been, the Costa Brava?' asked the sergeant.

'What, on police pay? I wish you'd give over. I was only on a few days' leave, any road. Went up to t'Lakes. Smashing weather. Ah, well, back to it, eh?' Collins turned and said: ''Evening, Mr. B.'

Bawtry smiled. 'Heard what you were saying. So you had a pleasant few days away from it all?'

'I did that.'

Half-jokingly, Bawtry said: 'You don't happen to have run across anyone from Hong Kong, I suppose?'

'Hong Kong?' Collins stared.

'It was just a stray remark. We're up a gum tree trying to find anybody who came to Liverpool from there, but . . . ' Bawtry stopped. A grin had come on the police driver's rugged face. 'What's funny about it, Bert?'

'Nothing, Mr. B.'

'Something made you grin.'

'I just remembered a thing that happened, before I went off on leave. Just a bit of a laugh.'

'What was it?'

'It's nowt, Mr. B, honest.'

'If it has anything to do with Hong Kong, however daft it seems to you, I want to hear it.'

Bert Collins looked uncomfortable. 'I'll be telling tales out of school . . . '

'You mean it concerns a friend of yours?'

'Well, yes.'

'He's been up to something?'

'Nothing illegal, sir, for God's sake.'

Bawtry said: 'I seem to be having more trouble interrogating one of our own officers than chatting-up villains like Big

Dave McTaggart or Ginger Ducie. What the devil's this all about?'

Collins made a sigh. 'It's just a joke. Well, all right, I'll tell you. I was driving back to Headquarters, it was the night before I went on leave, and this fella comes racing out of a side street carrying his shirt and jacket in one hand and his shoes in the other.'

'What fella?'

'I don't like mentioning his name.'

'It's a bloody order!' roared Bawtry.

'A chap in t'Merchant Navy, I've known him on and off a few years. Eddie Freeman, a good type.' Collins groped for cigarettes. 'He'd been out to some house. A bird he'd got to know invited him up. Well, all right, her old fella was away and Eddie was having it off with her.'

Joe Oldfield said: 'And then the husband returns unexpectedly and your mate does a bunk carrying his clothes, eh?'

'That's right, sarge.'

'I'm still waiting to find out where Hong Kong fits into it,' announced Bawtry.

'Well, it was like this: Eddie was with this married Judy when they hear a car turning into t'drive. Eddie just grabs his things and rushes out t'back. On his way through the lounge he caught sight of a photo and nearly had a fit on the spot because it was a picture of a fella he met in Hong Kong.'

'*When?*'

'He didn't say but it must've been a bit since because Eddie's been on short trips for some time.'

'How come he didn't spot this picture earlier?'

Collins grinned. 'Must've been too busy. But when he did spot it he got a right shock.'

'You mean it was a picture of this woman's husband?'

'As a matter of fact, it wasn't. Must be some relation or friend. It was a fella he knew as Langley . . . ' Collins broke off, staring.

'*God Almighty!*' breathed Bawtry.

Collins was looking from one to the other, bewildered.

Bawtry said thickly: 'This married

279

woman your mate was with — what's her name?'

'Eddie didn't say.'

'Where is he, then?'

'His ship sailed for Quebec next day, Mr. B.'

'Then we'll have to radio him . . . wait a minute, though, do you know the address of the house he went to?'

'Not the exact address, but I can tell you t'street he came pelting out of. Off Walton Hall Road it was, Holly Tree Crescent.' Collins fingered his jaw. 'I've heard that before, now I come to think about it.'

Bawtry didn't answer immediately. He stood there without movement, remembering that it was here, on this exact spot at Police Headquarters, that he had last heard the street name — The Bowers, Holly Tree Crescent, address of Mrs. M. Lancing who had run into Alison Raynes. He remembered something else; the odd tone in her voice when he asked if she was on her way home at the time. It was only a small thing but sometimes small things grew into bigger things, signposting the way ahead if you were reading the signs right. Was he? Not sure, but a picture was forming fast in his mind, sharply defined, the picture of a woman returning from a possible clandestine appointment and having a bump in a part of town she would not normally be in; that would explain the odd inflexion when she answered his question. Or would it? Just coincidence — no, it was too much of a bloody coincidence. Aloud he said: 'Did your pal say what his lady friend looked like?'

'He said she was a right smasher, a raving redhead . . . ' Collins stopped again. A curious expression came on his face. 'I've just thought of summat . . . '

Bawtry smiled faintly. 'You're a bit late, Bert, though not much.' He thought: I'm on to something at last. It's fantastic, a chance meeting. If I hadn't bothered chatting to Bert Collins I'd never have known — and if I hadn't stopped to have a drink with Bill Crawfurd I'd have missed Collins who would probably never have thought about the Eddie Freeman incident again.

He tipped his curly-brimmed hat off his forehead and said: 'You're just going on duty, aren't you?'

'That's right.'

'On the route taking in Walton Hall Road?'

'Why, yes.'

'You can drive me to The Bowers, Holly Tree Crescent,' said Bawtry.

21

Della Lancing showed him into the wide lounge and said: 'Is it something to do with the accident?'

'Just a routine call, ma'am. I thought you'd like to know that the girl you knocked down, Alison Raynes, is making a good recovery.'

'Oh? Well, I'm very glad.'

'Also that so far as the police are concerned there won't be any proceedings.'

Della smiled. 'I won't pretend that that doesn't make me even more glad, inspector.'

'Natural enough. Incidentally, Miss Raynes is the daughter of one of our officers.'

'Really?' Della sounded politely uninterested.

Looking at her, Bawtry thought: anything that doesn't directly concern this one won't interest her. She's a looker all right, though. Bert Collins's seagoing pal was doing himself well with another man's wife. Dissatisfied with her old fella, looking for a crafty bit on the side. Well-to-do middle-class, too much time on her hands. Must be marvellous in bed, not that I'm even remotely interested. I'm a one-woman man and I've got the only one I'll ever want, till death us do part and after that if it's possible. Something else — it's funny how apparently disconnected incidents are coming together on this case. Happen Toby Byass fits in somewhere. No, that's not likely. Or is it?

Bawtry became aware that Della Lancing was speaking again: 'It's most kind of you to take the trouble to call on me, Mr. Bawtry.'

'I just felt you were entitled to know the position and I was coming out this way in one of the police cars, Mrs. Lancing.' His gaze ranged casually round the room. He didn't want to ask outright to see the picture. Then he spotted it, on a low shelf in a corner beyond the vast fireplace.

He stood up, swinging his hat. 'Well, I'll be going, ma'am.' He took out a cigarette, picked up matches from the table and struck one, walking across the pale lambswool rug to drop it in the fireplace. The movement brought him close enough to see the picture distinctly.

It was the man who hummed the Merry Widow theme.

Over his shoulder Bawtry said: 'That's an excellent piece of photography, Mrs. Lancing.'

She shrugged. 'Yes, it's quite good.'

'I've a feeling that I've seen him somewhere. A friend of the family, eh?'

Della Lancing touched her vivid hair and said in surprise: 'Hardly — it's my husband.'

★ ★ ★

They were all in the shared office, a mid-evening conference when they were all due off, only now nobody was going off. Well, Brooker had gone out, but they knew which pub to telephone because he always used the same one for the first drink of the day, which was never before nightfall, though he made up for lost time then. He came back immediately, bringing a double whisky breath with him, and sat jingling coins in his trouser pocket.

Braxted said tersely: 'Right from the beginning, Sam — all of it. Facts, plain and unvarnished. Theories we can look at later.'

'Yes, sir.'

Bawtry ticked the facts off on his fingers, bringing everything out the way it had happened without pointing-up the facts in deliberate emphasis. They'd speak for themselves.

Fallon, ramming shag tobacco into his decrepit pipe, looked even more sadly long-faced than usual. Brooker sat on the edge of his chair as if he were about to spring off it. Braxted stayed impassive.

Nobody spoke till Bawtry finished and then not at once. It was Brooker who ended the small silence. '*We've got the bastard!*'

'Not yet.' This from Braxted, even-voiced.

Brooker paused in the act of lighting a cheroot. 'With respect, sir, it *must* be our man.'

'Almost certainly, but we still haven't sufficient evidence to justify an arrest.'

'But the name — Langley!'

'If Lancing claims it's a case of mis-identification what do we do?'

'It's enough to be going on with, surely, sir?'

'Enough to be going on with what — an arrest? We couldn't even get a committal for trial — unless we can bring Freeman into court to make a positive identification. Possibly not even then.'

Bawtry said: 'I've had another word with Collins, sir. He says Freeman was scared stiff in case his wife ever found out what he'd been up to. We'd have trouble getting him to testify.'

'He could be subpoenaed and treated as a hostile witness,' Brooker said. He grinned faintly. 'No, we haven't got enough on chummy-boy, not yet. But we'll book him all right in the end.'

Fallon took his pipe from his mouth and said gently: 'I've been watching you,

Sam. You're thinking of something, I can tell it.'

'Is there some fact you haven't told us?' Braxted fired the question like a bullet.

'I've given you all the facts as I know them, sir. There could be some theories arising from the facts.'

'Such as?'

'Lancing must have got into the bank, there can't be two men with a habit of humming *The Merry Widow*. Well, there could be, but the coincidence is too much in these particular circumstances. So far we've assumed that the bank intruder ran off because the watchman got free and sounded the alarm. I'm not satisfied with that.'

'Why?'

'I'm wondering if he merely wanted to see the layout of the bank and tied the watchman up loosely so that he *would* get free. In other words, it was planned to look as if the intruder took fright.'

Braxted said slowly: 'It's just a theory, but it could open up a new avenue. I'm not quite sure where it leads, though, unless he was setting the stage for someone else to do the actual robbery.'

'Somebody like Toby Byass,' said Brooker.

'It's possible.'

'But you don't fancy it as an idea, sir?'

'I can see Byass in the part — but, frankly, I simply don't see the necessity for Lancing to raid a bank.'

'His business could be on the verge of bankruptcy. That would supply a motive.'

'We don't know that and we've heard no rumours,' said Fallon.

'Well, we wouldn't, not in the ordinary way,' Brooker answered. 'Happen we'd better look into . . . '

The telephone rang. Braxted picked up the receiver and said: 'For you, Sam.'

Bawtry listened, making only small interpolations. When he was through he said: 'That was Dick Halloran. He says Matthew Lancing inherited a business under the terms of a will — and that he came here from Hong Kong getting along for a couple of years ago.'

'We're getting warm,' said Brooker. 'Anything else?'

'Yes. Halloran says the company is

highly prosperous but that there is a certain amount of unrest among shareholders about some aspects of the accounting system.'

'What aspects?' asked Braxted sharply.

'He doesn't know, but apparently a group of shareholders are calling an extraordinary general meeting.'

Brooker ground out his cheroot. 'That means time is running out for chummy. Happen he really *is* going to raid a bank in league with Toby Byass.'

'We could have Byass in for questioning, but if he refuses to talk all we'll have done is put Lancing on his guard. Besides, it's the Leng murder which really concerns us.'

'I'm certain Lancing is our man,' said Bawtry, 'but we need more evidence, such as having a bit of property when we're trying to prove a theft. In this case what we need is something to link Lancing directly with the murder.'

'Like what?' asked Brooker. 'Even if we could prove he was in possession of barbiturates it wouldn't do. Plenty of people have them these days. We seem to have become a nation of bloody pill swallowers.'

Bawtry looked round and said: 'I'm wondering if it'd be worth questioning any of the staff at Lancing's offices. One of them might have noticed something without realising its significance.'

'There'll not be anyone there at this time of night and by tomorrow Lancing'll be back.'

'His wife might know an address.'

'H'm — well, try if you like,' said Braxted. 'The only thing is it'll get back to Lancing.'

'Not necessarily, sir — or not in a form which would start him thinking. Depends how one goes about it.'

Brooker grinned. 'Depends on how Sam goes about it. There's nobody better at talking the madam.'

'A bit of kidology might work all right,' mused Fallon. 'Asking questions about one thing while trying to get the answer to another, eh?'

'Something like that, Ted.'

'I don't much care for handling a grave issue in this way — but, all right, see what you can find,' said Braxted. 'God knows we need to find something, and soon.'

Bawtry walked back into the C.I.D. room and dialled Della Lancing.

'Yes, Mr. Bawtry?'

'We're investigating a report that someone, a presumably unauthorised person, has been seen leaving your husband's place of business, Mrs. Lancing. There may be nothing in it, but we want to check. Specifically, we'd like to go into the offices — with a member of the staff.'

'Oh!' Again Bawtry thought the tone was slightly odd, not in the same way as before but odd.

'I take it all the staff will have gone home long since,' he said.

'Well, yes, I imagine so. The office closes at six, you know, but . . . ' There was a small hesitation, then she went on: 'Sometimes Mr. Fairfax, the chief clerk, works late, especially at this time of the year. You could try. If he isn't there you could ring his home. I don't know the number but he lives out at Norris Green — Mr. G. K. L. Fairfax.'

'Thanks, ma'am, you've been most helpful.' He hung up, waited a moment and rang the Lancing office number. Fairfax might not hear if the call went through to a switchboard. On the other hand, he might have left a line open to where he was working, if he *was* there.

The ringing tone went on for a few moments, then: 'Fairfax speaking, who's calling?'

Bawtry said who he was and repeated the story he had invented. 'I'd just like to come round for a security check, Mr. Fairfax.'

'Yes. Yes, of course. I'll let you in when you arrive.'

Less than ten minues later Bawtry was in the office. Fairfax had ledgers arranged on a desk under a shaded light. 'Just doing a bit of extra work,' he said.

Bawtry looked at him. He thought: the old-time faithful servant, not so many left these days, a dying race. Fifty years of meticulous service, overtime without thought of being paid for it. At the end of the road a few embarrassed words, a gold watch and a pension on a scale which meant you had to do without a summer holiday, go easy on shoe leather and keep the electric fire on one bar. Happen it wasn't that bad, though. A bit of brass tucked away, building society divi, tax paid, plus pension. It still wouldn't be a lot, though. Well, the police pension wasn't a fortune. I'd better save more.

'I hope I haven't alarmed you, Mr. Fairfax,' said Bawtry. The small deception of his visit had given him a slight feeling of guilt.

'A bit, yes, when you rang up — but it's all right now you're here, inspector.' Fairfax's gaze strayed to the books. 'I could finish my work while you look round, unless you wish me to accompany you.'

'No, I won't trouble you, Mr. Fairfax. I'll just make sure everything's all right, eh?' Bawtry smiled reassuringly.

'I haven't heard anything suspicious,' Fairfax said uncertainly. 'I hope nobody's got into the building.'

'If anyone has I'll know how to deal with him.' Bawtry started for the door, turned back and said casually: 'You haven't had any unusual callers, by any chance?'

'Today?'

'Any time in the last few days.' As he spoke Bawtry noticed the sudden expression on the other's face; a slight but unmistakable look of worry. '*Have you, Mr. Fairfax?*'

'Well, I don't know that . . . ' Fairfax fingered his shiny tie nervously.

'If you've anything to tell me it will be treated in the fullest confidence,' said Bawtry quietly.

The chief clerk hesitated. 'It . . . it's nothing, really.'

'Except that you're a little troubled about it, whatever it is, aren't you?'

'I . . . I wouldn't like it to get back, to Mr. Lancing I mean.'

'It won't, Mr. Fairfax. But if there *is* something bothering you it might be better to tell me.'

'Yes, I suppose so.' Fairfax blinked. 'It can't possibly have anything to do with your visit here, unless he's come back.'

'Unless who's come back?'

'A man who was here the other night.

I'd better explain. I was working a bit late or going to when Mr. Lancing came and said I could go. I thought . . . well, I thought he was anxious for me to go, if you follow my meaning.'

Bawtry nodded, not speaking. Better not to interrupt, not yet. Something was coming, he could feel it.

Fairfax said: 'I'd got half-way to my bus stop when I remembered I'd left something behind, something my wife asked me to get during my lunch break, so I went back. I was surprised to hear voices coming from Mr. Lancing's room. I didn't want to eavesdrop and I couldn't catch it properly, anyway — but I heard a voice, a man's voice, asking for five hundred pounds down and two hundred a month. That's what I heard as I came in. This man also said he wanted to be taken on the payroll, but it didn't sound like a candidate being interviewed because of something else.'

'What?' Bawtry asked the question without raising his voice.

'The man said he didn't mean to do any work, not so's you'd notice, and then he said 'I just want to keep an eye on you, *Mister* Lancing' — that's exactly how it sounded.'

'And then?'

'I didn't hear any more, all I could think of was getting away, I was terrified of Mr. Lancing finding out I'd come back.'

'This voice you heard, did you recognise it?'

'No, I'd never heard it before.'

'Can you describe it, what it sounded like? The accent or anything that struck you about it.'

'Well, it was a bit unusual, sort of a sing-song voice.' Fairfax stared. 'Why, do you know him?'

'We're making inquiries about a man with a sing-song voice.'

Fairfax made a small gasp. 'Why, it might be the man seen hanging around here, the very man you came about, Mr. Bawtry.'

'It might. A fella with nearly blue-black hair . . . ' Bawtry stopped. 'What's to do, have you thought of something?'

'I was going to tell you, I waited about

for a bit, I didn't like the idea of the boss being with this man.'

'I thought all you could think of was getting away.'

'Yes, but I couldn't do it. I waited behind a door, sort of to see that everything was all right. Then Mr. Lancing came out with him. I had a narrow view, but I could see he had very dark hair, almost blue-black like you said.'

Bawtry stopped the breath rustling from him. 'And after that?'

'Why, they just got in Mr. Lancing's car. They didn't see me, I kept out of sight I was that scared of the boss thinking I'd been prying. I hadn't, I'd no intention of it, Mr. Bawtry.'

'I'm sure you hadn't. Apart from his dark hair, did you make anything of this visitor?'

Fairfax seemed to hesitate, then said: 'To tell you the truth, I thought he was a little drunk.'

Bawtry felt a tightness inside him. 'What made you think that, Mr. Fairfax?'

'He seemed a bit unsteady and Mr. Lancing had to help him into the car. In the back, not the front. He *must* have been intoxicated, inspector, because he sort of slumped down out of sight . . . '

Fairfax peered over his slipped bifocals. 'Is . . . is that important in some way?'

'More than you know,' said Bawtry.

He ranged from room to room, missing nothing, then walked fast back to Headquarters.

Brooker swung round as he strode in.

'The International Commercial Bank's been raided again,' he said.

'Has it?' said Bawtry, almost buoyantly.

22

Telephone calls brought Braxted and Fallon from their homes, interrupted half-way through late dinners they weren't going to finish now. Braxted arrived looking as nearly animated as he ever permitted anyone to see. Fallon came two minutes later wearing a shaggy tweed sports jacket fraying at the cuffs; no time to change back into his suit, not that the suit was much smarter.

Brooker said: 'Tom Varley's handling it C.I.D.-wise. He's just been on the blower. Says nothing's been taken, no money missing — yet there was tons of the stuff. We wouldn't have known there'd *been* a raid except by chance. Fred Lewis was driving a panda past the place and saw a light, shouldn't have been one. Night watchman locked up — they banged a door behind him. Intruder or intruders unseen and now vanished.'

'So we don't know whether or not Toby

Byass had anything to do with it,' said Fallon.

'No.'

'I thought we were supposed to be watching him,' said Braxted.

'So we were, but he managed to dodge the d-c we put on his tail. I've sent Lucas after him, not that it'll do any good. Toby'll alibi himself and he won't have any bank money because none was taken.'

Braxted said reflectively: 'That's strange.'

'Bloody baffling,' rumbled Brooker. 'I don't get it.' He set fire to a cheroot. 'Sam's news is more important, though.'

Bawtry made everything sharply explicit. When he was through Braxted said: 'It's good work, but there's one thing more.'

'Yes, sir, Lancing's car. No matter what he's done about cleaning it up we'll find something that connects with Leng.'

'It wasn't on the parking ground behind his office, of course.'

'No, it'll either be at the airport or, more probably, in the garage at his home.'

'We'd better look at it,' remarked

301

Fallon. 'If we find anything, even a fibre strand from Leng's clothing will be enough, we'll be ready for a confrontation the moment Lancing steps off the plane tomorrow. The only thing is, we don't want to alarm his wife in case she rings him up about it.'

'You know the make, colour and registration, I take it?' asked Braxted.

'Yes, sir. A two-litre Daimler, 1970, dark blue, Liverpool registration.' Bawtry gave the combination and added: 'I'll have the airport police check the parking ground and call us back.'

He put the call through and hung up. The telephone rang almost immediately. It was Lucas. Braxted listened and said, aside: 'Byass hasn't returned home.'

'In some boozer,' said Brooker. 'I know most of the ones he uses. I'll get Information to radio all cars to make spot checks on their routes.'

The airport police came back on the line: 'Daimler, 1970 model, registration and colour as described, parked here. Do you want us to move it?'

Braxted said: 'Impound is the word. We

want to examine it inside and out, particularly inside. Leave everything in it just as it is.'

'Right, sir.'

Brooker moved a finger upwards along the left side of his jaw, making a small sound because his face needed a second shave.

Fallon took his pipe from a sagging pocket. 'If the lab mob don't find anything in the car I take it we still go ahead?'

'Yes.' The Chief Superintendent smiled. 'Perhaps a little less confidently, though Fairfax's story is significant enough to bring Lancing in for questioning.'

'There'll be *something* in the car, sir,' said Bawtry. 'Also, I found barbiturates under the private bar in his office. That's not conclusive — but we'll probably find Leng's dabs there, on the desk most likely.'

'We've taken Leng's, posthumously. No criminal record in this country. We're still waiting for Hong Kong to report. Should be here by morning. Not that it matters greatly.' Braxted eyed Bawtry for a

303

moment, then said: 'You went to Lancing's office ostensibly just for a casual chat with anyone on the staff who might be there. I think you already had a different idea.'

'More a hope than an idea, sir. I reasoned that there was a chance, perhaps more than a chance, that Lancing would interview Leng in his office — after everyone had gone so that there would be no danger of being seen or heard. But there was also a faint chance that someone on the staff might have stayed on a few minutes, enough to notice something.'

'You kept that notion to yourself . . . ' began Braxted.

Brooker chuckled. 'Sam's still a bit of a loner.'

'Police work is a combined operation linking a number of men of differing ranks and skills,' intoned Braxted. Without change of voice he added: 'However, it's results that count in the end, very little else.'

It was a tribute and Bawtry understood that, but he thought: one day I may go it alone and fall down on the job and he'll wipe the floor with me. Well, I'll take that chance.

But he merely said: 'I had luck, sir. If Fairfax hadn't noticed that Lancing was anxious for him to go and, more particularly, if he hadn't gone back looking for something he'd forgotten I wouldn't have been able to draw him out — there wouldn't have been anything *to* draw.'

'In which case we might not have heard about your ideas,' observed Braxted amiably. 'As to luck, that often consists in being in the right place at the right time. You were.'

Brooker, jingling coins again, said: 'What about Lancing and Toby Byass? There's something damned peculiar going on, a fella getting into a bank and not touching anything.'

'Not touching money,' put in Fallon.

'If it was Toby all he'd be interested in is brass. That could mean being paid a lot of money by Lancing to get something different out of the bank.' Brooker was looking hard at Bawtry as he spoke. 'That means something to you, doesn't it, Sam.'

'It's possible.'

Braxted looked edgy. 'If you're keeping something else back . . . '

Bawtry said slowly: 'When I was with Lancing's wife I had an impression that she was worried about something.'

'Well, that's not surprising,' Braxted said. 'She may know or suspect what her husband has been up to. Also, he may know or suspect what *she's* been up to.'

'Yes.'

Brooker interjected: 'I've asked Tom Varley to see if anything other than money is missing. Like some document or other.'

'Yes,' said Bawtry again.

Braxted steepled his fingers. 'Not just some document — a particular document?'

Bawtry started to speak: 'I think . . . ' Then the telephone sounded again. Fallon grabbed it this time. His over-long face suddenly went tight.

'Now what?' demanded Braxted testily.

'The airport police say the Daimler is

no longer in the car park,' announced Fallon.

'Christ,' said Brooker. 'That's all we needed, a bloody car stealer snitching the evidence from under our noses.'

Fallon was still on the line. Bawtry said: 'Ask if a flight has just come in from London, Ted.'

The Superintendent spoke down the mouthpiece. Then, turning his head: 'They say yes, ten minutes since.'

Brooker stood up fast, jamming his hat on his grizzled head. 'God Almighty, that means . . . '

'Yes,' said Bawtry.

23

Matt Lancing slid down behind the wheel of the Daimler, turned the ignition on and listened to the soft purr of the big engine. He nearly purred along with it. Everything was moving inexorably to its appointed end — appointed by Matt Lancing, no chance of a slip-up anywhere now. He had called Toby Byass at a public telephone kiosk near Everton Valley at a prearranged time, an untraceable STD call from another kiosk at Heathrow.

'I got it, boss,' Toby had wheezed triumphantly. 'See you in t'Green Acres eleven-thirty tomorrow a.m., then?'

'We'll do better than that, Mr. Byass. I'll pick you up where you are now — tonight, ten-thirty at the call-box.'

'Great, I can pass the time having one or two.'

'You do that, Mr. Byass. Five grand for you and the document for me when we meet. You made the switch, of course?'

'Yeh, I made it.'

It was 8.15 p.m. when he phoned Toby. Then he rang his home. It was necessary to make sure Della was in and not going out again. There was a flight to Speke at 8.50. He would be on it. By 11.30 at the latest he'd be driving through the night back to London and when the hotel chambermaid brought his morning tea he'd be in bed to take it. Nobody would know he hadn't been there all night. The perfect alibi — look at it how you liked, you couldn't fault it.

Only he *would* have been absent, up to Liverpool and back again and the daily maid would find Della dead in bed and scream for a doctor. Overdose of sleeping tablets, presence of alcohol in bloodstream. Very sad. Verdict: misadventure. Or was it accidental death? Who cares? By the day after the funeral he'd be in Switzerland, opening four numbered accounts one after the other. And long before the extraordinary general meeting he'd have vanished without trace. Airline tickets to distant places, original identity, then a new one backed up by a new passport, a subtly applied suntan, dark hair rinsed to ash grey. Going south, then east or west. A long way off, that was all that mattered.

And now he was back in Liverpool, driving unhurriedly home, savouring his triumph. A hogskin brief-case lay on the rear seats stuffed with money. Ten minutes later, after a fleeting stop, it was empty. Pity he'd had to part with five grand to that fat bastard of a safe-breaker. He had even considered killing Toby Byass, but had changed his mind. What he had got was worth the money and if Toby ever talked it would be too late, much too late.

But he had to kill Della. It wasn't just that she had gone whoring around; she knew too much, that was why he had had to get the document out of the safety deposit. Well, it was done. Cost him five thousand that had, plus the risk in hiring Byass. Well, she was going to pay for it, for that and the other thing. He had loved her, had wanted her as his wife — until he found out what she was doing behind his back. He'd have divorced her or simply left her, but she'd made that impossible, the bitch. Even though he'd got the document she could still talk, still make trouble for him. She knew about the numbered accounts and if he simply disappeared she'd guess what had happened and set the coppers on him. Well, she wasn't going to have the chance.

He drove on, up St. Domingo Road, crossing Everton Valley and on into Walton Road, heading for The Drive and finally the little crescent off Walton Hall Avenue. Nine fifty-nine p.m., a clear night with a full moon, make driving back to London easy. What he had to do first wouldn't be easy, but he would do it just the same, it was necessary. I don't want to kill her, but I'm going to. The last act, the final wiping-out of the past. If she wasn't in the mood for gin there was always coffee, loaded with soluble barbiturates. Suppose the taste put her off and she refused to drink it, suspecting him? It wouldn't save her because he would use the gun he had brought with him, a silenced .32 Smith and Wesson; he didn't want to, but he would.

Matt made the left turn and rolled into the drive of their fine home. Lights showed downstairs, from the big lounge. She was up, reading or watching television, not with a boy friend; he'd made sure of that.

He got out of the Daimler, crossed leisurely to the wide porch with its brass-bound coach-lamp and let himself in.

★ ★ ★

Della heard the car and then the key turning in the lock. In her heightened awareness the small sound was almost like a thunderclap. The door closed and she called out, faintly: 'Is that you, Matt?'

'Of course, who else?'

He came into the lounge, smiling. A tall, handsome man, impeccably dressed, chairman and managing director, the synthesis of executive achievement and masculine charm. She thought: God, I hate him.

'I didn't expect you back tonight,' she said.

312

'Bit of a surprise, darling. I finished unexpectedly early and just had time to ring you before I caught the plane.' He walked to the private bar. 'Drink?'

'All right, gin and tonic.' She watched him while he made two.

Over his shoulder he said urbanely: 'I was quite surprised myself, finishing early.'

'Everything went all right, then?'

'The business meeting, you mean?'

'Of course, what else?'

He stood with his back to the fireplace, facing her on the white lambswool rug, his legs straddled apart. 'The business meeting was nothing, really.'

'Oh?'

'No, I've got something else to tell you.'

'I thought you might have, Matt,' she said composedly.

'Did you now? You're a very perceptive woman. I wonder how perceptive.'

'I don't know exactly what you're going to tell me, Matt — but I'll make a guess.'

'Do.'

'I think you're getting ready to pull out.'

'Well, well!'

'You are, aren't you?' She finished the drink.

'Another?'

'Why not?' She watched him again while he got two more.

He turned and said: 'It was a good guess, but you don't know the details.'

Della ran a naked arm along the back of the settee, looking up at him. 'I heard a whisper today that a group of shareholders are asking for an extraordinary general meeting. I'm guessing that it's a meeting you have no intention whatever of presiding over.'

'You *are* smart,' he said admiringly. 'Do you mind telling me the basis for that assumption?'

'You told me, a long time ago when things were different between us, that you had money invested abroad. When I found out about those numbered accounts I didn't have to be that smart to guess that you'd multiplied the sum many times over. You've now got to the point at which discovery is imminent. Would that be a fair deduction?'

'I love the way you put it, darling.' He swirled gin round in his glass. 'Who told you about the shareholders getting ideas?'

'Connie Enders.'

'That jolly-hockey-sticks nymphomaniac? What does she know?'

'Just that some shareholders want a meeting, she doesn't know why. George told her.'

'Somebody ought to tell *him* something.'

'Perhaps he already knows.'

'I suppose it's possible. Turning blind eye hoping phase will pass, you mean?' He shrugged. 'But I was going to give you the details. They can be condensed into a sentence — three hundred thousand pounds waiting for us, my sweet.'

'Us?'

'But of course. We leave tonight. I've seats booked for us both on the one a.m. flight to Zurich.' He promoted a look of mild surprise on his handsome face. 'Don't tell me you aren't coming!'

'I'll have to come, won't I, Matt? I can't stay on here without money.'

'I was hoping there might be a better

reason. Perhaps a new life together.'

Della crossed her legs. 'You had it made here, why didn't you settle for that?'

'Darling, you're slipping. Sooner or later there was always the risk of being found out. Some small mischance, anything.'

'Don't call me darling, Matt.'

'Why not?'

'Because you don't mean it.'

'Oh, but I do. I always have — despite everything.'

'All you care about is money, Matt — in this case all the company money you've put away in those numbered accounts.'

'Embezzled is the right word, we don't have to pretend. And that's not all.'

'No?'

'I'm not even legally entitled to the position I have, not even the name you know me by. I usurped the inheritance . . .'

For a long moment she didn't speak. Then: 'I didn't know that, but it explains something I've felt was wrong about you lately.'

'I'll tell you everything when we're safely on the plane. There isn't time now. Meanwhile, you can reflect on the fact that you've shared it all with me.'

'I'm your wife, I live here in the home you provided, I knew nothing except what you told me.'

His face went tight. Then he laughed. 'My, my — you're trying to appear respectable. That's a good word, after what you've done to me.'

'Yet you still want me to come with you, wherever you're planning on going.'

'Yes, I want it. I'm not giving you up, I want you.'

'How flattering!'

'I want you at my side, a new life together, Della. Let's drink to it.'

'I've already had two and they felt like trebles.'

'Why not? We're celebrating.'

'One more then, and not so strong this time.'

'As you say.'

She lay back in the settee, her face turned from him as he crossed to the miniature bar, his back to her. Quick, now, in case she turns this way. He carried the two glasses and put them down carefully on the coffee table, one each to hand.

'Bottoms up, then!'

She was reaching for hers when she said suddenly: 'What's that?'

'What?'

'I thought I heard something. In the hall.'

His head jerked round automatically. 'You're imagining things, darling.'

'Just the wind, perhaps. All right — down the hatch in one, for me.' She drained the glass and put it down, looking at him.

He laughed gaily, raising the other glass. It's all over, I've done it, everything's . . .

The door opened and Sam Bawtry walked in.

24

Matt Lancing wheeled completely round, then stood transfixed with the glass almost at his mouth. Words tumbled madly through his brain, but he was incapable of speech, aware only of engulfing panic and a dull thunder paining his ears.

'The joke's over, Mr. Lancing.'

He scarcely heard the words. They were drowned by the screaming torment of his stretched nerves. Even his vision was hazed, so that for moments he could see nothing beyond the flickering bulk of the man before him; but that was more than enough.

A voice sounded, like a strange muffled voice heard a long way off.

'I beg your pardon . . . ' It was his own voice, it had to be because his lips were phrasing the words.

'I must ask you to accompany me to Police Headquarters . . . '

The haze eddied and cleared. He stared at the big man in front of him.

Bawtry . . .

That's the one who was in the bar, I recognised him and went out because I didn't want to be seen with Toby Byass. But I didn't think anything else of it because he couldn't possibly know anything. That's what I thought, I was sure of it, but now he's here with his bloody police jargon. All my perfect plans, what's gone wrong, how *could* they go wrong? They couldn't. I know they couldn't. But he's here, he's come here for me.

Brooker came through the doorway. 'I've phoned Headquarters. The finger-print and forensic fellas are on the way to look the Daimler over.'

The car . . . they must expect to find something. They won't, though. I wiped all the surfaces, over and again. Suppose there's something else? God, I didn't think of anything except fingerprints.

Matt put his untasted glass down on the table. As suddenly as the panic had come it had gone. Della Lancing was sitting rigid, staring at him, but he didn't even glance back. He was looking at the door. There was freedom out there; they hadn't got him yet.

He heard his voice again, deep and smooth now. 'I'm afraid I haven't the foggiest notion of what this is all about, inspector. D'you mind explaining?'

Bawtry said levelly: 'I must ask you to accompany me to Police Headquarters to assist in inquiries we are making into the murder of Thomas Leng . . . '

Leng! So they knew. Jesus Christ, how did they know? It didn't matter, nothing mattered now except freedom, freedom only a few feet away. I can make it, I'm going to make it now.

His right hand made a sweeping movement inside his swung-open jacket. He went sideways, very fast, bringing the silenced gun out in an almost unseen blur. Simultaneously, Bawtry dived. They banged down, locked together, rolling over and over.

Bawtry drove a knee upwards. Lancing made a hard dry screech, but he still had the gun. He tore himself free, aiming.

Bawtry lunged at an angle away from the muted blast, then hurled himself forward. The gun spun across the floor. Matt went after it, one hand clawing.

A foot slammed hard down on his wrist, crunching on it. Brooker's foot. Car tyres slapped the gravelled drive. Booted feet thudded and the room seemed full of uniformed men.

'Put handcuffs on chummy,' Brooker said. He took a cheroot out, looked at it and put it away. 'Your prisoner, Sam — you'd better charge him.'

'Presently,' said Bawtry.

Della Lancing was standing without movement, as if stunned into immobility. Matt Lancing stared down at his manacled hands, then looked up and laughed. It was like no laugh they had ever heard.

Two uniformed constables led him away. Brooker started after them, paused and said softly: 'Back in say five minutes, Sam . . . '

A small silence seemed to hang in the still air. Bawtry shifted his weight and said: 'It will be necessary for you to answer some questions, Mrs. Lancing.'

The stunned look left her. It hadn't been genuine, not even for an instant, and he knew it.

'I'm not clear what you mean, Mr. Bawtry.'

'I think you may be in a position to throw some light on certain factors in this case.'

'You referred to a murder, what could I possibly tell you about that?'

'Not about that, Mrs. Lancing. About your husband's business — specifically, the probability of large-scale embezzlement and falsification of accounts.'

'So you overheard?'

'Enough.'

'I didn't know police officers eavesdropped.' She made a sneer of the statement.

'It's necessary sometimes,' he answered impassively.

Della took a cigarette from a silver box and tapped it on an enamelled thumbnail. 'I have precisely nothing to tell you, Mr. Bawtry,' she said coolly.

Bawtry looked at her — a handsome,

sophisticated woman in command of her emotions, still scheming while her husband faced a life sentence. But she wasn't going to get away with it.

'I think you have, Mrs. Lancing. In particular, I believe you can help us trace the numbered accounts where your husband has transferred stolen money.'

Della lit the cigarette with an onyx lighter, a deliberate slow-motion action. She blew the small flame out and said: 'I'm afraid you are optimistic, inspector. I don't know the numbers.'

'I think you do, I'm positive that you do.'

'Really, Mr. Bawtry! I suspected only recently that my husband has such accounts — I do *not* know their location or any details whatever.' She smiled. 'He was — well, somewhat secretive.'

'I can hold you as a material witness, Mrs. Lancing.'

'Aren't you overlooking the fact that a wife cannot be required to testify against her husband?'

'If you are keeping back information which could lead to the recovery of a large sum of stolen money we may be able to think of something.'

'You're using words without an exact meaning. Are you trying to intimidate me?'

'I don't think you are a woman who could easily be intimidated, Mrs. Lancing.'

'Thank you.'

'But what I do think is that you are in actual possession of the numbers and are considering gaining access to the money, either in the near future or at a later date.'

'You'll find that hard to prove, inspector.'

'I can't prove it,' answered Bawtry calmly. 'If you maintain complete silence on the point I can't even stop you leaving the country.'

'Then perhaps you will be kind enough to leave me with my personal grief.'

Bawtry said steadily: 'We have reason to believe that your husband, in association with another man, took something from a safety deposit at the International Commercial Bank.' He let the words stay in the air for a moment, watching. A flicker came into her eyes and went away, nothing more.

'I'm guessing that you put something in the safety deposit, perhaps something which incriminated your husband and that for reasons of his own he had to get it.'

Still she said nothing, Bawtry looked down at the coffee table. 'I'm sorry if I'm intruding on your personal grief. Perhaps you'd better have that drink your husband left.'

'Why not?' She picked up the glass, smiling inwardly. Oh, I'm clever all right, this policeman isn't going to get anywhere with me. She put the glass to her lips, then took it away, as if she were about to speak again.

Bawtry said distinctly: 'I saw you change the glasses round when you pretended to hear a sound in the hall.'

The triumph left her. She moved a tongue suddenly dry.

'Your husband killed a man named Leng by administering drink and drugs, a massive overdose of soluble barbiturates on top of liquor.'

'What has all that to do with me?'

'I think your husband got possession of something which incriminated him and came here to kill you in exactly the same way. Only you guessed — happen more than guessed — and simply switched the glasses round.'

'How melodramatic!'

'If there *was* something in that glass and your husband had drunk it he'd be unconscious by now and soon he would be dead, just like Tom Leng. Very sad — also very difficult to explain how a man planning to flee the country voluntarily took a lethal dose.'

'What a sensational story you're making up,' she mocked. Her gaze darted to a boxed plant in the window bay.

'If I am then no harm can come to you from that drink you're holding, Mrs. Lancing.'

'None whatever, but I don't think I'll bother after all.'

She moved very fast, but not so fast as Bawtry. His fingers closed on her wrist like a vice, rock-steady. He took the glass from her and stepped back.

For a moment she stood perfectly still, looking at him. Almost in a whisper she said: 'You bloody bastard, you.'

Bawtry said nothing.

She picked up her cigarette, then abruptly pitched it into the hearth. 'Well, what are you going to do — charge me with the attempted murder of my husband?'

'I could make it stick, Mrs. Lancing. I have the evidence you were about to pour away.'

'It'd be your word against mine, wouldn't it? No corroborative evidence.'

'Nevertheless, you'd be in a rather disagreeable position.' He smiled bleakly. 'Do you want me to charge you?'

She looked at him again, a long bitter look. 'No.' This time the word was scarcely a whisper.

Bawtry didn't speak.

Slowly, Della said: 'Suppose I tell you what you want to know?'

'I'll need more than just telling.'

She slid a hand down the cleavage of her dress and handed him an envelope. It was warm. 'It's a copy of what was in the safety deposit . . . '

Bawtry opened the envelope, saw what was inside and put it in his breast pocket. He picked up the glass again, crossed the room and tilted it into the boxed plant.

When he turned back she said: 'You know what you've done, don't you? You've just deprived me of a fortune.'

Bawtry swung his hat against his side. 'You've got something in exchange, Mrs. Lancing — rather more than you deserve.'

He went out.

★   ★   ★

The final conference. Braxted in a rare expansive humour. Brooker encamped behind yet another cheroot. Fallon's face seemingly not quite so long as usual.

Bawtry made his report. There was one omission.

They went through the facts. Braxted rose. 'Still things to tie up. Detailed forensic tests on Lancing's car. Examination of the firm's accounts. New contact with the police in Hong Kong. A lot to do.' He stifled a yawn. 'We'll get down to it in the morning. Fortunate you were able to obtain a copy of the numbered accounts, Sam.'

'Yes, sir. They were in the house.'

Braxted made a bleak smile. 'Lancing failed to take into account the possibility that his wife would make a copy of what was in the safety deposit.'

'Yes, sir.' Bawtry thought: he'd have found it all right after he poisoned her, only she nearly poisoned him instead. Ah, well. Aloud, he said: 'Lucas is seeing Toby Byass, though it'll not be easy to prove he went into the bank if he keeps his mouth shut and he will.'

'Except that Lancing's already implicated him.'

'We'll need more than his word, sir.'

'You'll have to do a masterly job of interrogation, then.'

'I'll try,' said Bawtry. He walked back into the C.I.D. room with Brooker. It was late and they had it to themselves.

Brooker said casually: 'I let you be alone with Della Lancing, I sensed that's what you wanted. How'd you manage to make her give you those numbers, Sam?'

'A bit of persuasion.'

'Like what?'

Bawtry told him.

'Well, Lancing meant to kill her — not that it justifies her trying to kill him,' said Brooker. 'Might've been difficult getting a conviction against her, though, but you didn't tell her that, of course — and you got those numbers.' Brooker made a sound that was not quite a chuckle. 'Just the same, Braxted would scream ten thousand murders if he knew what you've done.'

'Are you going to tell him?'

'Who, me? I didn't hear what you said, Sam,' replied Brooker imperturbably.

It was long past midnight when Bawtry went home to Carol. She came close in between his arms, then pushed him from her.

'You're tired, I can tell. But there's something about you — that look, I know it. You've finished the case.'

'*We've* finished it.'

'I'll bet you had a lot to do with it.'

'I don't know how I ever got along

without you to boost my ego.'

'You'd always get along, that I'm sure of. But I like to think that you get along better by having me.'

Sam grinned. '*That's* a thought!'

'Samuel Dennistoun Bawtry, don't you ever think of anything except that?'

'Yes, eating. I'm hungry.'

'You shouldn't eat late at night.'

'I won't, then.'

'Oh, but you'll have to now, I've got something ready.'

He reached for her, kissing her mouth, her neck. Carol struggled free and said: 'Wasn't there something in the paper the other day about kissing being dangerous?'

'Yes, some German fella claims that young girls have died from heart attacks due to body changes brought about just by kissing.'

'I'm not a young girl, but if kissing causes all that I shudder to think what takes place if you go a bit further.'

She slid her hand into his, swinging them together and looking up at him. 'If we get over-excited we might both die of heart failure right in the middle of you-know-what.'

'It'd be a nice way to go,' he said.

Carol laughed and they walked hand-in-hand through the lounge and the door closed behind them.

THE END

THE GUILTY WITNESSES

John Newton Chance

Jonathan Blake had become involved in finding out just who had stolen a precious statuette. A gang of amateurs had so clever a plot that they had attracted the attention of a group of international spies, who habitually used amateurs as guide dogs to secret places of treasure and other things. Then, of course, the amateurs were disposed of. Jonathan Blake found himself being shot at because the guide dogs had lost their way . . .